ONCE WE ARE SAFE

A Novel

I0761252

ALESSANDRA CARATI

TRANSLATED BY LINDA WORRELL AND LAURA MASINI

This is a work of fiction. Names, characters, organizations, places, events, and incidents are either products of the author's imagination or are used fictitiously. Any resemblance to actual persons, living or dead, or actual events is purely coincidental.

Text by Alessandra Carati, copyright © 2021 by Mondadori Libri S.p.A.
Translation copyright © 2025 by Linda Worrell and Laura Masini
All rights reserved.

No part of this book may be reproduced, or stored in a retrieval system, or transmitted in any form or by any means, electronic, mechanical, photocopying, recording, or otherwise, without express written permission of the publisher.

Previously published as *E poi saremo salvi* by Mondadori in Italy in 2021. Translated from Italian by Linda Worrell and Laura Masini. First published in English by Amazon Crossing in 2025.

Published by Amazon Crossing, Seattle
www.apub.com

Amazon, the Amazon logo, and Amazon Crossing are trademarks of Amazon.com, Inc., or its affiliates.

EU product safety contact:
Amazon Media EU S. à r.l.
38, avenue John F. Kennedy, L-1855 Luxembourg
amazonpublishing-gpsr@amazon.com

ISBN-13: 9781662534294 (paperback)
ISBN-13: 9781662528828 (digital)

Cover design by Ploy Siripant
Cover image: © traumlichtfabrik / Getty

Printed in the United States of America

to my father, the polar star
to my mother, the root
to Belma

I.

THE ESCAPE

APRIL 1992

1

The one memory from my childhood that stands out, unimpaired, is a forewarning of what would later happen.

Our life was simple, ending where the village ended, framed by the woods, the road leading into town, and the orchards climbing up the mountain. Beyond those boundaries, there was no other world where we could imagine living.

Mirko and I were six. We played where we pleased and were inseparable, two peas in a pod.

One day, while sitting outside my house, Mirko said, "The war is coming, and we'll have to leave."

We didn't know what war was. Just a word murmured in hushed tones that had the power to make the grown-ups jittery and mean.

I stood up and shouted at him, "The war is *not* coming, and we are *not* leaving."

Mirko stood up too. "It *is* coming. Either we leave or we get killed!"

He couldn't hit me, so he bundled all that frustration into his balled-up fists and ran off. Then he threw himself on the hens pecking nearby, causing them to flee in all directions, like frightened spiders scampering out of a hole.

At home, I asked my mother if it was true that the war was coming. "No," she said, "it will never come to this village."

I believed her.

2

"Stay awake."

The heat from the stove had filled the whole room, and I'd dozed off.

"Don't fall asleep." And this time, my mother shook my shoulders.

"I can't stay awake."

"Keep your eyes on the door. They could arrive any minute." In the dark, I searched for the light filtering through the doorway.

We all slept in one room, on mats on the floor. My father was building a larger house, just for us, but it wasn't finished yet, so we were living with my grandparents. Aunt Mejra and my cousin Samir, two years younger than I was, were staying there too.

Whenever my milk was boiling on the stove, Samir would plead with our granddad for some, until he got half. Not that Granddad didn't love me, but Samir was a boy, and in our village a male child was worth more. My mother grew angry, so Grandma secretly added water to my portion. Once, I ended up in the hospital with diarrhea. My mother took Grandma aside and said, "Don't ever do that again."

Then she steeled herself and spoke to Granddad. "The milk is for my little girl." It was brave of her; she was younger than I am now, with fewer opinions and desires, and had always felt like a guest in her own life. I came to appreciate this much later, after years of anger, after horror had swept away any meaning and left us exhausted creatures on the ground.

I heard my mother rummaging through our things, trying to pack whatever she could. Grandma was helping her, and when she cried, they hugged.

"Where are you going to go? You've got everything here. The freezer is full of meat and vegetables. You're better off staying."

"Your son told me to go. If in a week things have calmed down, I'll be happy to return, but for now I've got to leave."

My father was working abroad. Whenever he came home, he'd bring new dolls, so beautiful they looked real. There were none like them in the village, so I immediately buried them in the garden, in a secret place. They were my hidden treasures, and no one was allowed to touch them, not Samir, not Mirko, not any of the other children in the village.

Babo had told Mamma on the phone, "Go to the registry and get the deed to the house and the land. Your documents and the child's. And the photos. Leave everything else."

He would be waiting for us on the other side. He couldn't pick us up, because soon the borders would close, so we had to make the journey alone. My mother was pregnant.

Grandma brought me a cup of coffee.

"Have a sip, *kuća moja mila*." She called me "my dear little house," the phrase for "my little love" in our country. She only said this when we were alone; it was our special thing. I took a sip of the coffee; it was so bitter I wanted to spit it out, but I didn't know where and gulped it down instead.

Then the door burst open.

The sound made me freeze. I stood motionless, staring at the dark silhouette framed by the light.

"We've got to go. Now."

It was Granddad's voice. And our hearts started to beat again.

"I still need to get a couple things for the child."

Granddad looked at my mother. "There's no time, Fatima; they're coming."

3

We left at night, the frosty grass crackling under our feet. April can still be very cold in our country. My mother turned to look at the house, then put her hand on my shoulder. "Say goodbye to your grandma." I have no memories of that moment, no memories of the warmth of Grandma's cheek against mine, her clear pale eyes, or the musty smell of hay on her clothes.

In no time, we were in the dense brush of the woods, Granddad in front with Samir on his shoulders, holding my aunt by the hand, Mamma and me behind them. We made our way through the undergrowth, over the fallen tree trunks, as the animals scurried to and fro, their sleep disturbed. It was cold and dark, and I was scared.

"Mamma, where are we going?"

"To meet Babo."

"Where is he?"

"Across the border."

I was out of breath and didn't ask any more questions. The woods had always been off limits to us kids; we looked at them from afar, enchanted and intimidated. And now my mother was suddenly dragging me through the tangle of branches. My feet sank into the soft moss, clods of dirt stuck to my shoes, and each step became more difficult.

Her hand yanked me forward and then pulled me back, as if we had to run but didn't know where to go. We stopped. She looked around. Granddad had disappeared; we could no longer see his figure leading the way.

A rustling grew louder than any other sound. We instantly crouched down, and she covered my mouth with her hand, wrapping herself around me. I could feel my heart pounding through my body.

The silence returned; whatever had come for us was gone. The only noise in that stillness was the pee streaming down my leg and dripping onto the wet bark. I was melting, turning into water that could flow to my grandma, and she'd send me to sleep with the story of the old fat sheep that escaped death disguised as a wolf. I curled up, wrapped in a cocoon of anger, and prayed to Allah to punish my mother for dragging me out of bed.

"Fatima."

For a second time, Granddad's voice saved us.

"If you lag so far behind, you and the child will be the first ones they catch."

I wanted to tell him that he had scared the life out of us, that he was carrying only my cousin on his shoulders and Mamma was pregnant and lugging a heavy backpack, that I had little legs and we'd been left behind because he had forgotten us. If we'd been caught, it would have been his fault. But Granddad was already ahead of us, and if we didn't follow, the woods would swallow him up again.

While I was walking, the cold damp fabric of my pants rubbed against my legs. Who knows if Mamma had noticed that I'd wet myself. Since leaving home, she'd never even given me a hug.

We climbed up and down the hills, and I hoped every crest would be the last. I tried to keep up with everyone, my eyes on the ground, saying nothing, asking nothing. I'd never seen them so scared. I didn't know it then, but time was the only thing we had left. Granddad was carrying Samir in his arms and constantly checking to see if we were following.

Suddenly, we were out in the open; there was a road lined with houses below, a parking lot crowded with people and three waiting buses.

Granddad turned and looked at us as if he thought he were seeing things, but we were there in flesh and blood, exhausted. He put my cousin on the ground and drew closer, staring at us with a dazed look in his eyes, like he only then realized that we'd walked eight miles in the dark.

He kissed my mother's hands and pressed them against his cheek. "Forgive me, Fatima, forgive me." Then he grabbed hold of me to put me on his shoulders.

"No, we're here now." Mamma kept walking toward the parking lot, dragging me along. She wasn't angry, just desperate and in a hurry.

Granddad shoved ahead and shouted to make himself heard. He pulled a wad of banknotes from his pocket to buy our tickets. Finally, we climbed on board, the two of us in front, my aunt and my cousin behind. But without Granddad. He would return to the village.

We didn't even hug goodbye. Everyone kept saying that it wouldn't be for long—two weeks at most, and then we'd go home.

The bus pulled away slowly. Granddad watched us from below, placing his left hand on his heart, his palm open wide in our country's ancient sign of farewell. He closed his eyes, and when he reopened them, he looked only at my mother.

4

Everyone was talking loudly, the men smoking. My mother pulled me closer, and I snuggled under her arm, resting a hand on her belly. Grandma had told me that's where I'd come from too. I wondered if Granddad was already home with her.

When we reached the town, it was still dark, and yet throngs of people were everywhere, dragging enormous bags, crowding around the departing buses and shouting.

Mamma was holding a piece of paper with the address of one of Granddad's cousins.

"Hurry up, Mejra, and keep your son next to you."

My aunt looked stunned, like a child thrown into an amusement park. My mother grabbed her arm and pulled her along with a strength I didn't know she had.

Our cousin's house was small and tidy, with a telephone near the entrance and a TV that was much bigger than ours. As soon as we arrived, my mother took off my clothes and gave me a bath, like she'd done when I was little. I can still remember the sense of relief I felt.

She washed me with a foamy soap, and shiny clusters of bubbles slid onto my thighs, arms, and stomach. Some were big, others very small, and all twinkling like tiny, faraway lights. It was my first time in a bathtub, with hot water. In our village, the women collected water from the well, and it was always ice cold, like freshly melted snow. I liked going with them; they would fill their jugs and buckets and then sit on the stone walls. They took off their *šalče*, the scarves they wore to cover their heads, and talked of their husbands and children, of when they were girls. Some sneaked a cigarette. They laughed, and I couldn't wait to join in the world depicted by their words. Even now, I think the little girl leaning over that well is another child, my double, stuck in a life far removed, on the other side of the woods.

~

We stayed in hiding for days. Our cousin's husband was sick, and she had to look after him, so we only saw her when she checked whether we had enough to eat and were warm during the night.

Samir and I always stayed inside while my mother and aunt went out to search for a way to leave. My mother said that everyone wanted to flee. My aunt said that she was tired and wanted to return to the village. In the evening, they would put us to bed and then watch the news on TV. I stayed awake to listen in secret and often recognized a man's voice threatening "I warn you, you are condemning your people to hell. You are not prepared for war. You are facing extinction."

I'd only heard that word once before, in a documentary about dinosaurs. After the extinction, nothing was left of them, not even their babies. I started to tremble under the blankets.

Someone turned off the TV. We could just make out the hum of the refrigerator until my aunt spoke up. "Those things are happening in the capital, not at home."

"Mejra, Tarik is waiting for you at the border."

"Why didn't he come pick me up?" she whined.

"Don't be silly, don't you know what they're doing to the men? They're taking them away. Do you want that to happen to your husband?"

I heard my aunt whimpering.

My mother snapped at her, "Do as you like. I'll do what my husband told me to do."

"Fatima, I'm scared; I want to go back to the village."

"Did you hear what Granddad said on the phone? The day we ran away, they blocked the streets. No one can go in or out anymore."

"They came, and they will leave."

"They're the Chetniks, not the federal troops. And they are everywhere."

A long silence, and then the door to our room opened. I closed my eyes. My mother lifted the blankets; the cold chilled my skin, but it faded away when she lay down beside me. She always slept in her clothes, the backpack next to the door, ready.

5

She came running into the house, without even taking off her shoes or her *šalče*. My aunt was preparing dinner in the other room. Samir and I were watching *The Simpsons*, lying on the floor like two puppies.

"I've got the tickets." My mother looked at us, excited and out of breath, while she showed us four small pieces of crumpled paper.

Homer was rescuing Springfield from a nuclear disaster by randomly pushing buttons on his keyboard.

"Where's your aunt?"

I pointed to the kitchen without taking my eyes off the screen.

"Mejra, we've got the tickets; we can leave."

"When?"

"Now."

My aunt kept peeling the potatoes, staring at her hands.

"Did you hear me?" Mamma yanked her arm.

"Let go of me," she said through clenched teeth.

"You have a son; it's not just about you."

"Those buses are dangerous! There are checkpoints everywhere. They're pulling people off and taking them away."

"If you don't want to come with us, fine. But you and the child have got to stay here. For a while." My mother's voice was calm again, distant, as if my aunt and Samir were no longer her responsibility.

"I'm not like you, I'm not . . ."

I couldn't figure out whether she wanted to cry or hoped that my mother would take pity on her.

"Promise me you'll stay here."

My aunt sniffled and nodded.

We gathered our things and stuffed them into the backpack and in no time were at the door, quickly hugging without looking at one another. We were frightened, and fear devoured all other feelings. I held my cousin tightly, nipped the solid flesh of his chubby cheek, then bit him harder. He squealed, pushing me away, and burst out laughing.

On the lane outside the house, I turned around. Aunt Mejra was holding Samir in her arms; they were watching us. I blew them a kiss with all my breath and heard my cousin call out, "Aida!"

We were already on the road, walking away quickly. Before new memories lodged in my heart, I asked, "Mamma, am I going to see Samir again?"

"Of course."

"When?"

"I don't know."

"Where?"

She paused. "Somewhere."

6

My mother was quarreling with the driver. He didn't want to let us get on, saying there was no more room. People crowded around the door, and I felt like I was suffocating.

We were squeezed on board by the people pushing from behind. The driver closed the doors. The ones outside kept trying to pry them open, but he started the engine and pulled away. People were clinging to the windows or the side mirrors; some were walking on the roof. Their bodies were hurled into the air; we left them and their screams behind. The bus sped up, and finally the last few dropped off, one by one. I watched as they collapsed on the ground with dull thuds or cracking sounds that made me shudder.

"Mamma, did they get hurt?"

She didn't reply; she was trying to figure out where we could sit. Whole families were crammed into one seat or stretched out on the overhead racks or lying on the floor. We could do nothing but stay where we were, on the steps. My mother had one hand on her stomach and the other around my shoulder. I thought of Samir in his warm bed with Aunt Mejra and wanted to cry, but I felt ashamed in front of all those people.

"Why didn't we stay in town?" I asked, holding back waves of sadness.

"Because your father told us to leave." She was staring at her shoes.

Crushed together, cheek by jowl, we tried to fall asleep and dispel our fears. Once out of town and off the main road, the bus carried on slowly, following the back roads that passed through the villages. We stopped, drank water from the wells, ate whatever was at hand, whatever the farmers would give us. We came to a river on the border. The bridge had been blown up, so we got off the bus and boarded a boat and then another bus.

My mother was shaking. "I don't have our papers." She was rummaging nervously through her handbag, looking for something that wasn't there.

Things were so chaotic that no one asked any questions. The guards let everyone pass quickly, in big groups, without even looking at us. My mother was still shaking, and I thought of the baby in her belly. Who knew if I would love that baby the way I loved Samir, if I could love anyone the way I loved him.

On the second bus we found a free seat. Next to us, an old man kept repeating, "Soon they'll close everything. Put up barbed wire and checkpoints to make sure no one leaves."

I couldn't take my eyes off him.

"Mamma," I whispered in her ear. "How will Samir and Aunt Mejra get to us, and Grandma and Granddad, if they put up barbed wire?"

"Go to sleep, now." I knew she wouldn't say another word.

7

Beyond the window, the landscape had changed: an empty plain devoid of trees and a dull sun that made us sweat. A strange gaiety had been spreading through the bus. My mother told me it wouldn't be long—at dawn we'd reach the final border.

"And then we'll be safe."

That's what she said, safe. The old man had dozed off with his head against my back. I was trying to move as little as possible, to avoid waking him. It was our last night on the bus.

I'd fallen asleep, and when I opened my eyes, I saw my mother staring into the darkness. The air was filled with a stale, heavy smell. I couldn't breathe.

"I need to go to the toilet." I tapped her hand. She didn't move. "I've got to go."

"We can't stop. You need to wait." I kept quiet and looked out the window, like she was doing. "Can you hold it?"

Before I could reply, the bus jerked, abruptly lurched forward, and came to a halt. Shafts of light blinded me. I grabbed my mother's cold, still body. A woman screamed; a dull thump silenced her; everyone held their breath. Then, a man's voice.

"Get off, one at a time, in single file. And keep quiet."

Beams from the flashlights struck us. The orders and the sound of boots and weapons were coming from all directions, turning the darkness into solid matter charged with danger. We crashed blindly into one another and crowded together to shield ourselves from danger, like the newborn mice that Granddad kept in a box.

"Nothing will happen if you do as we say." It was the same voice, young and shrill. "We're not here to hurt you."

I could see them, in their dark clothes, carrying rifles, pistols, clubs. They were just kids. The one in charge spoke calmly. "Women on this side and men in a line over there. Don't rush, and keep quiet."

We separated, unclasping our hands, caressing each other's cheeks, women refusing to leave their sons. A man with a weapon grabbed the wrist of a child in their mother's arms; she shouted and struggled, but the soldier wouldn't let go. The woman bit his hand, as if wanting to rip his flesh from the bones. A wild scream from the man's mouth, a punch to the woman's face, and the thud of her felled body.

I closed my eyes and pressed my face against my mother's legs. While I was counting and hoping that someone would come to help us, the man in charge curtly fired off an order three times in a row, "Only boys over twelve!"

He looked around furiously, to make sure it was carried out.

"No rough stuff," he growled.

I looked at my mother; her eyes were glassy. She wasn't speaking; it didn't even seem that she was breathing, and if she wasn't, neither was the baby. I took a deep breath, as if the air could flow all the way to them.

We walked in orderly lines as directed, to a point not far from the bus. My mother wouldn't stop squeezing my hand, her grip like an iron clamp. The woman next to us whispered, "At twelve, they still have smooth cheeks, skinny legs. Twelve is nothing."

The men, about thirty feet away, were watching us. We stood waiting until some headlights appeared at the end of the road. Once the women understood what was happening, they flung themselves at their sons and fathers and husbands but were pushed back by rifles and clubs.

My mother wrapped her arms around me. "Close your eyes and pray." Her embrace was so strong that nothing could hurt me. I was protected by her voice and the soothing litany of the Koran.

The soldiers forced the men onto the trucks, pushing and shoving them, threatening them. The women's despair roused all the animals on the plain, but to no avail. Eventually, the soldiers climbed aboard the last truck and cleared out. Only the driver was left, his head hanging over the steering wheel as he sobbed in the darkness.

The women got up, a single mass of sorrow moving through the night with their *šalče* and long skirts. Their weeping grew into a chant that accompanied them onto the bus. We had to continue our journey; there were children like me and young and old women, and though no one dared say it, the war had found us.

A lady in an elegant jacket with a sparkling brooch said to my mother, "They'll take them to work in the fields, and when it's all over, they'll come home."

"They will," Mamma replied.

"They will," the woman repeated.

Before climbing on the bus, I tugged at my mother's skirt. "I need to go to the toilet."

"Can't you hold it?"

I shook my head.

She grabbed my arm and pulled me along the road, to a spot where the vegetation was low and dense. "Hurry up."

I ventured a few steps forward, just behind a bush, and looked up: two dark eyes were staring at me; a machine gun glistened in the moonlight. I screamed. A young soldier, his face painted black, jumped out of the twisted mass of branches, shouting angrily and pointing the gun at me. I raised my head and, as the stars started to spin, fell to the ground. My mother stifled a cry and threw herself onto me. The scene unfolded slowly, in silence. Only the sensation of the grass embracing me, her warm body on top of mine, and the damp earth below. Plunging, gliding toward a radiant point floating in the darkness. Back in my bed, with Samir sleeping, breathing, dreaming next to me. The smell of his milky skin everywhere. I was dead, and death was pleasant and soothing.

"My love, my sweet little girl."

I opened my eyes; the stars were motionless, fixed in the dark sky. I remembered the black hole of the gun barrel and started to shake. My mother was cradling me in her arms.

"I'm here. I'm holding you."

We stood up. The soldier had vanished into the plain.

8

We sat in the front of the half-emptied bus, near the driver. He glanced in the rearview mirror, started the engine, and returned to the road, driving as if in a funeral procession. Not a sound emerged from the back, but the women were awake, even the elderly ones. Their eyes frantic, their jaws clenched, some crying in silence.

My father must be alive and waiting for us at the border. My mother had fallen asleep. When I'd thought I was dead, all that was most dear to me—our village, my bed, Samir—appeared before my eyes, and now I longed to be dead again. While praying to Allah to let me die, I fell asleep too.

It was nearly daybreak when I woke up, and the landscape had changed again: hills, woods, small villages along the road. Maybe time had traveled backward and erased the past few days. My chest swelled with joy, and I stood on the seat to look for the tip of the minaret, the giant beech guarding the road that climbs to the village, my granddad's fruit trees. My eyes scanned the countryside; the view looked the same, yet nothing felt familiar.

Suddenly, a woman in the back screamed, pointing at a spot on the escarpment below us. I leaned forward and saw an overturned bus, full of people. A child was trying to climb out from a broken window, his head drenched in blood.

My mother covered my eyes and took me in her arms. "Stay here, and don't move."

The child, his blood, the screams rising from the slope below had no effect on me. Deep inside, my life had dried up.

A young woman lunged toward the driver. “Stop!”

He stepped on the gas.

Then other voices shouted, “There are people in that bus.”

The young woman drew closer, but the driver kept his eyes on the road. “Ladies, they're gonna close the borders. Don't know about you, but I wanna save my ass.”

They fell silent and went back to their seats. We were in a race against time, with room only for desperation and, often, cruelty.

When we reached Ljubljana, the sun was high above us. As the bus moved through the city, someone complained because they wanted to get off. The driver said, “Cities aren't safe; we're headin' straight for the border.”

There was some grumbling, and then nothing.

“Aida, do you need to go to the toilet?”

“No.”

“Are you sure?”

“Yes.”

My mother was staring at me. “You know, girls who don't poop can die.”

“That's not true.” I no longer believed her.

I turned to the window. We were passing over a wide, placid river. I had no idea there were bridges that could link two banks so far apart. There were tall buildings everywhere, casting shadows on us. The war couldn't come here; these beautiful things couldn't be destroyed. We would return to our village; my most precious toys were buried there. Believing this, I had no need to hold on to anything or say goodbye.

When we got past Ljubljana, we'd been traveling for three nights and four days.

We'd soon reach the border.

The women busied themselves, looking for a change of clothes, documents, money. My mother raised her sweater and took out a plastic bag hidden under her top; inside were her identity card from Tito's Yugoslavia, a wad of bills, and a handwritten note from my father. Only a few lines, capital letters and some numbers.

She held the note in her hand, stroking it, drew it to her chest, then turned to ask the young woman sitting behind us to lean forward. "What does it say?"

The woman reached for the note, but my mother wouldn't let go, so she was forced to bend closer to get a better look. "It's an address."

"What's the address?"

"Prešeren Square." She hesitated. "It's the main square in Ljubljana."

My mother looked at her. "That's not possible," she whispered, her lips growing pale. "Read it again." She stood up and stuck the note under the girl's nose.

"Why didn't you get off in Ljubljana if that's the address written on the note?"

Because Mamma couldn't read.

"Where are we going?" she asked.

"To Sežana; that's where the border is."

My mother slumped into her seat, like a rag doll. "How will I let him know that I'm in Sežana? How will he find us?"

She was crying softly. A vise gripped my throat. The only thing in my world that was keeping me afloat, the only thing that had yet to disappear over the horizon, was now sinking to the bottom of the sea.

"Don't cry," I said and rested my head on her tummy.

She laid her hand on my hair, and her caresses calmed us both. "We'll be fine, Aida."

She sang me a *sevdah*, a folk song that tells of the Drina, our wide swollen river that divides the world into two. A boy on one bank, and a girl on the opposite; they are in love but cannot touch, only gaze at one another from afar. Finally, after much suffering, they discover a secret ford.

"We'll find a secret passage too, and meet Babo again," I said.

"Kuća moja mila." With my mother's words, Grandma's face, her voice, filled my whole body.

9

The bus came to a halt in a large square close to the customs house. As soon as the driver opened the doors, the women rushed off, clutching their documents. We sat on a low concrete wall that divided the square from a playground. My mother watched the people coming and going, clinging to the backpack that held all our belongings. In an endless line, women and men were trying to cross the border, many in cars, a lot on foot like us. All around, entire families had set up camp; mattresses, sleeping bags, and cookstoves were everywhere.

"Mamma, what are we doing?"

"We're waiting."

"Waiting for what?"

"I don't know."

I grumbled.

"*Nafaka*, Aida."

Like all Bosnians, my mother was a fatalist. In life, you may have very little, but you endure, you make do. Then the time comes when even that little bit is gone and there's nothing left, and at that very moment, something turns up out of nowhere, from someone you don't even know. When that happens, we say it's *nafaka*.

"Can I go play over there?"

"No, sit here next to me."

"Why?"

"It's too chaotic. And because I said so."

She was scared, like an animal venturing out of its cage for the first time. I looked at the toes of my shoes, my socks, my pants. The same as when we'd left. While swinging my legs back and forth, I shot from the wall and there I was, in the playground. I felt energized, revived. I was taking deep breaths, jumping, running, diving into the grass.

My mother had climbed over the wall and was running toward me. "Aida! Come back here!"

I hid behind a slide. She tried to grab hold of me as I kept running. She was struggling, frightened and tired, but I didn't want to sit still any longer.

Before slipping away, I caught sight of a man quickly coming toward us. He had a black mustache and wasn't smiling. When he reached my mother, he said, "Fatima." She looked at him. She was pale and sweating.

"Are you Fatima?"

She covered her belly with her hands.

"Damir sent me."

The sound of my father's name made her jump. "Where is he?" she asked in one breath.

"In Ljubljana. He's coming. He told me to take you to the hotel and wait for him there."

I saw the look in her eyes. She was trying to understand, to cling to a sliver of hope, as she wondered whether to trust him.

"I'm the owner of the hotel, that one next to the customs house. Do you see it?" He pointed to a low-rise concrete building. "Damir has already paid for your room and board and everything else you might need."

"How did you pick me out among all these people?"

"I heard you call your child. Damir told me that his daughter's name is Aida."

"What else did he tell you?"

"Nothing much, only that you were coming from the Drina and he's taking you to Italy."

No one had ever told me I'd be going to Italy. I didn't know a thing about Italy except what the village women would say when we got into trouble: "You little rascals, may Allah send you to Italy!" Since we'd behaved like scoundrels, we deserved to end up in a land of scoundrels.

My mother took my hand. We crossed the playground and made our way through the camp. Tents as far as the eye could see, a shouting, desperate expanse of humanity. As we were walking, the man told us that things were getting worse; too many people had arrived, and every day it was harder to get through; it might take weeks of waiting before they'd be able to cross the border. Most didn't have their papers in order and were sent away, so they would wait for the shifts to change and try again with the next police officer. It all depended on him; if he had a good heart, they could go over even without documents. And so every day, people tried to get across, always in a line. Agony. But this was about to end too, because they'd soon be closing all the crossings, he was sure, and then it would be hell. He was ready to leave if he could go with his whole family.

"This is no longer the country I loved. I'm the sort of man who still takes his hat off in front of Tito's image. I can't help it." He spoke without regret. It was a fact, and that was that.

My mother had been sorry to leave our village; I remembered the way she'd watched our house fade into the darkness and disappear as we entered the woods. She had not cried or spoken or even kissed Grandma. Sadness was a poison building up in our bodies.

10

The room had brown carpeting everywhere, even in the bathroom. I immediately plopped my head on the pillows of the double bed. They smelled of fresh linens. I couldn't wait to get undressed and slip under the covers. For the first time in days we felt safe; our fears had eased, giving way to exhaustion. Suddenly, I felt sleepy.

"You have to get cleaned up first."

I followed my mother to the bathroom, and, in one fell swoop, she sat me on the toilet.

"Let go of me!" I screamed while I squirmed, trying to get away.

"We're staying here until you poop."

Tears streamed down my face and wouldn't stop. Who knows when I'd started to cry. I was grabbing onto her shoulders; she was on her knees, facing me, and holding me down.

"I don't want to!" I kept saying through my sobs.

She gave me a confused look, then her grip turned into an embrace. "Just relax."

She stroked my head and whispered softly in my ear. As my body jerked and trembled, I again saw the soldier's rabid eyes, his gun pointed at me, and the stilled stars above my head. She took me in her arms and cradled me like a small child, the way my aunt did with Samir. As I sank into her warm body, my pain merged with hers. I closed my eyes, forgetting the madness and terror of the past days.

11

At dinner, I ate everything they put on my plate: a frittata with potatoes and cheese, hot soup, stewed meat. Mamma was eating too and, at times, smiling.

"When will Babo come?"

"Tomorrow, I think."

"Do you think he'll bring some dolls?"

"I don't know." She held her breath for a moment. "I don't think so." She grew serious again, lost in thought.

As we went up to our room, I could barely keep my eyes open. Maybe I'd eaten too much, or maybe it was the heat; it was very hot in that hotel.

"You have to go to the bathroom before you go to bed." Her voice was firm. I didn't struggle as she sat me on the toilet and filled the sink with hot water. She took a small enema out of her skirt pocket. I looked at it, knowing what it was. Aunt Mejra had used one once with Samir. I was paralyzed with fear.

"It won't hurt, and afterward you'll feel better." She caressed my cheek while she explained that she didn't know how long we'd be traveling, so it would be best to empty my bowels now. Her words "empty your bowels" bounced around in my head. I put my hands over my ears as if that would protect me from what was about to happen. She did what she had to, and I couldn't hold anything back.

As I let myself go, I burst into tears and dug my nails into her cheeks. The drain was swallowing the village, my cousin, our races through the cornfield, my grandparents, the tip of the minaret, the old sheep in the fairy tale. My world had disappeared, the only world I had ever known, the only world I had ever loved.

When Mamma put me to bed, I was exhausted. I no longer cared where we would go or even if we would survive.

12

"Wake up."

She touched my bare arm, poking out from under the sheet.

"Don't you want to go play?"

If it's a nice day, I thought, *I can go down to the stream with the other kids and roll stones into the water.* I opened my eyes. My mother had a blanket around her shoulders like someone who'd survived a shipwreck. Brown carpeting covered everything. Then I remembered where we were and turned over.

"Do you want to go on the swing in the playground?"

I looked at her.

"The owner of the hotel told me that Babo called; he'll be here tonight." Her face lit up. "The two of us can have some fun until he arrives."

She'd gotten some rest and was smiling. Outside the window, the camp looked like an enormous anthill; people were busying themselves collecting water and cooking, someone was singing, women were running after their children and scolding them loudly. The line to cross the border was already long and had come to a standstill.

"I want to go home," I said. "Nobody can get past there. Can't you see?"

"We won't need to stand in line like the others."

"But we don't have papers either."

"Your father will have sorted things out, I'm sure."

"Then where is he?"

"Enough of this. Get dressed, and let's go down for breakfast."

Her tone had changed, as if a chill had wafted into the room. My mother had always been like that, capable at times of being incredibly harsh. Those moments came without warning, with not even a cloud to let you know a storm was closing in.

At the playground, I met some kids, two brothers who'd been at the border for ten days. We were taking turns on the swing, and I wanted them to push me harder.

"Higher!" I urged them on.

One of the two said, "We're going to Germany," as if he'd suddenly remembered.

"Where is Germany?" I yelled from the swing.

"I don't know, but my cousins and grandfather are already there."

I looked at them, wondering if Italy really was the place where bad kids were sent. I hoped not.

"Why don't you come too?"

"I'm going back home."

They burst out laughing. "That's impossible! There's no going back. They'll kill you with machine guns; the ones who stay behind are going to die."

And once again, I could see the child with the bloodied head who had tried to crawl out of the bus window.

"That's not true," I shouted and jumped off the swing, falling on the gravel. They watched me, their eyes wide. My knees were bleeding. I hurled myself at the older one and knocked him to the ground.

"Get off me!" he yelled. "And you idiot, help me!"

His brother stood still; my mother was trying to drag me away. "Aida, are you crazy?"

I didn't let go and managed to give him a couple of slaps before feeling a strong hand clutching my neck.

"Tell him you're sorry."

I turned, fired up and ready to fight, to pour out all my anger and fear. Then I saw him. I sprang to my feet, wanting to get closer, but he held me at a distance.

"Tell him you're sorry."

"Babo," I managed to say as tears streamed down my face.

"Tell him you're sorry," he repeated.

I turned toward the boy, still on the ground. "Sorry," I said without even looking at him. The two brothers ran away, and I rushed to Babo.

He wrapped his arms around Mamma and me. She was pressing her hands on his face to make sure he was real, or maybe she feared he might leave again. The outside world, alien and hostile, was losing definition and fading away. In my father's hands, everything would be all right.

We sat on a bench; he cleaned my knees with his handkerchief and told us how he'd waited at Ljubljana and heard that a bus had gone off an escarpment and overturned and that no one had survived. In a state of despair, his head had started to spin; he thought he'd lost us forever. Then he phoned the cousin we'd stayed with in town, but the lines were always going dead, and it had taken him several hours to finally get through. He asked when we'd left, trying to figure out if we might have taken a different bus, and eventually convinced himself that we must have been on the later one; anything else was unbearable.

While he spoke, he looked at us, touching our hands, our faces, our legs, and his eyes quivered with emotion and excitement.

"I was sure you were somewhere, alive, waiting for me. I sat on the ground in Ljubljana, in the square, among the people shouting, and as I was retracing your journey in my head, I remembered telling you about Sežana and the border, and it dawned on me that maybe you'd made your way here. When they called last night to tell me you were safe, I went off to get drunk because my happiness was so great it could have killed me."

We walked away, hand in hand, my father in the middle, my mother and I on either side. From behind, we looked like a family, one of the many ready to cross the border.

13

"I've got to find a way to get you across."

My father was confident, smiling. Even the carpet in the room seemed less oppressive now that we were all together.

My mother handed him the plastic bag she'd kept hidden under her skirt throughout the journey. "Here's my identity card and Aida's paper."

"They won't be of much use to us, Fatima."

Mamma's identity card was from a country that no longer existed, and mine was just a slip of paper without even a photo, hastily produced by the Red Cross a few days before we left the village.

Babo checked every paragraph in the deed to the house and the land. We didn't know whether that piece of paper would be important in a few months. Then he saw the photos.

"Did you only take three?"

He was turning them over in his hands; one was of me and Grandma, the other two of my grandparents together.

"It was dark, and we had to hurry."

"All I asked you to do was get the documents and the photographs." He had raised his voice.

"Damir, the photos are at home; we can get them when we go back."

He stood up. "I have my passport and residency permit for Italy, but I can't take you with me because your documents aren't valid." My mother looked at him. "When I picked up Uncle Tarik to take him across, he didn't have proper documents either. A man helped us, right here in Sežana."

"How much does he want?" she asked.

"Nothing. When I tried to give him some money, he slapped my hand." He added, "He's one of us. He works here and is helping lots of people get out."

"What's he risking?"

My father said nothing, and his unspoken words echoed through the room.

My mother closed her eyes. "I didn't realize we were already so desperate."

Out the window, the mass of people seethed like a rough, threatening sea.

"I waited too long to tell you to come."

"And Mejra? How will she manage with her child?"

"Mejra was a fool. Tarik is furious."

"She's young."

"So are you."

"She was frightened."

Babo looked at her, a sudden twinkle in his eyes as he acknowledged the courage and determination that had brought us here. He sat alongside her and placed his hand on her stomach, caressing it gently.

"And Mejra? And Samir?" she asked anxiously.

"We're getting organized." He stood up and placed his left hand on his heart. I was gripped by the memory of Granddad. "I'll be back soon."

My mother turned toward me. *Don't be afraid; it's almost over,* she seemed to be saying.

14

The roar of the cars drowned out all other sounds, and the exhaust fumes made the air unbreathable. I'd never seen so many, a traffic jam that spontaneously fell into orderly rows. In the distance, the border guards.

"Evening is the best time. They're tired, full of food, and slightly drunk," the man said to my father. He never addressed Mamma or me. I was expecting a superhero, like the one I'd seen in Mirko's comic books, but I found myself standing in front of a small, skinny man who could have been a teenager if not for the white hair on his temples. He was constantly smoking. "Did you bring what I told you?"

"Yes, everything's in their backpack."

When Babo had come back to the hotel, he'd given Mamma a pair of glasses and me a hat with a visor. Then he'd said, "You'll wear your *šalče*, so nothing looks unusual."

He'd made us sit on the bed and went over what we had to do three times.

"You'll get in the car with him; at the border he'll hand over three passports: his, his wife's, and his daughter's. Try not to look nervous and don't do anything strange and everything will be fine."

"It's a secret mission," I said, and my mother stroked my head, then covered her eyes with her hand. Babo helped her stand up. "Fatima, we're nearly there." She burst into tears.

~

"Are you ready?" the man asked.

"Yes," said Babo. I'd already pulled my hat on.

"You'll cross on your own. Go as far as Trieste and stop at the last service station before the city."

My father nodded, then took my mother's hand.

For the first time, the man spoke to us. "Come on, jump in."

His calm tone did not reveal what he was feeling. Before getting in the car, he approached my father and gave him a piece of paper. "If something goes wrong, call this number."

As we were leaving, I turned to look out the rear window. Babo didn't wave; he only closed his eyes. My mother, in the front seat, put on her glasses and looked straight ahead.

At the border, the line of cars was moving slowly. The sun was setting over the horizon.

"Your names are Lejla and Vesna," he said, first pointing to Mamma and then to me. "Come on, repeat it."

My mother stared at the man through her thick glasses.

"Repeat it," he said again, patiently.

"My name's Aida, not Vesna." I looked at him in the rearview mirror.

"Do you like the name Vesna?"

I thought about it. "Yes."

"Good, so as long as you're in this car, your name will be Vesna." He turned to look at Mamma. "Missus, are you okay?"

My mother's body contracted in a spasm, her hands clutching her thighs, as if she were afraid of being swept away by a gust of wind. The journey, the fatigue, the perseverance would all have been for naught without one more small miracle. I knew what Mamma was doing; she was silently praying.

"Come on, tell me your name."

She was so frightened she couldn't speak.

"I've already taken lots of people across. Trust me."

They were just the right words because her body sank into the seat, she loosened her grip, and her breathing returned to normal.

When only a few cars were in front of us, the man stuck his head out the window to get a better view of the guardhouse. He turned his eyes back to the street and said, "I know them; they're good people. It's our lucky day."

My mother lowered her head.

Only one car ahead of us and then it would be our turn.

The driver in front of us had crammed lots of things into his car. The luggage rack was so full that the rear end almost touched the ground; inside, the heads of four teenagers sprouted up between the bags. The car lurched and came to a halt. He handed the documents to the police officer, who fixed his eyes on the faces of the woman and the man behind the wheel before leaving the guardhouse to shine his flashlight on the boys. He motioned to his partner to join him. They talked to one another in low voices; the smaller one lit a cigarette.

We waited, motionless. The light had changed; the sky was darkening.

"And now?" my mother asked, in a voice so faint it sounded as though she were speaking from the bottom of a well.

"It's easier to cross after they've stopped someone."

Looking back, I'm still struck by the coldness of that man. One day, Grandma let me touch a snake she'd caught in the garden, and I'd immediately pulled my hand back; it was silky smooth, and cold, like the fruit jelly she gave us as a snack. "Snakes are like that," Grandma had explained. "They warm up if they're next to something warm." Maybe that man was like those snakes.

The officers motioned to the car in front of us to follow them. The driver put it in gear and drove slowly behind the two men in uniform. The post was unguarded, the road ahead free.

My mother turned and, motioning with her head, urged the man to drive on.

He understood immediately. "Are you crazy? Do you want to get us shot?"

"It's dark. They won't be able to see us."

They didn't have time to say anything more because two new policemen arrived. They were young and seemed a bit excited.

"Passports," the bigger one said loudly as he approached the car. The man handed them through the window, open, one on top of the other. The officer looked at the first one and then at the man's face, did the same with my mother and finally with me. Although the evening was cooling off, the road seemed to be on fire, spewing heat into the car.

"Take your hat off."

I immediately did as I was told and looked straight at him. He rested his arm on the window and stuck his head into the car. He reeked of alcohol and tobacco.

"I thought you were a boy with that cap on your head," he said caustically. I kept quiet and lowered my eyes, because I didn't want him to see how angry I was. Mamma retched and put a hand over her mouth.

"She's pregnant," our man said.

Whether it was because of my reaction or the baby in her stomach, the officer backed away and threw the passports at us.

"Clear off!" he said without even looking at us. "Next time, I'm going to arrest you, you dickhead." He'd shouted at us, but his voice sounded far away because we were already over the border.

I pulled my hat on again. My mother leaned her head back and closed her eyes. The man lit a cigarette.

The last part of the journey was quick, like a door being slammed shut. In no time, we reached the parking lot. I saw my father in the cone of light cast over the gas pump, suspended in that glowing bubble, and rubbed my eyes because I thought he was a mirage.

"Here's your husband," the man said to my mother, and for the first time he spoke gently.

He pulled the car into the shadows. She got out, and Babo was already standing there, ready to help her. I stayed in the car, watching them.

"And you, aren't you going?" the man asked.

I looked at him from under my visor. "Aren't you coming with us?"

"No, I'm heading back."

I took my hat off and gave it to him. "For the other kids."

His eyes narrowed as he smiled. While I was waving goodbye, he slowly drove off, then he disappeared.

We would cross the border many a time after that, but would never see him again and would even forget his name.

We never thanked him.

II.

THE FAMILY

1992/1993

15

Upon our arrival, we were assigned a house in a town on the outskirts south of Milan. We shared it with Uncle Tarik and five other families, all refugees. The building was divided so that each family had their own small apartment, two rooms overlooking a concrete quadrangle shared with a bank.

The courtyard immediately became our territory. There were thirteen of us, "the gang of kids." We spent all day there, drawing with chalk, playing four square, setting up a net to face off in games of volleyball or football, some getting into fights and beating each other up. The bank employees watched us from behind the windows, like fish in an aquarium. At that time, the courtyard seemed immense. Some months ago, I passed by and saw that it was no more than nine hundred square feet, just a patch of concrete.

A fat Bosnian woman wearing a *šalče* with a portable radio playing at full blast kept an eye on us. She sat in a folding plastic chair, and we thought that one day she would break it; just the idea made us laugh like crazy. It was a happy life, and soon I got used to it.

For the Feast of Sacrifice, we got hold of a sheep and kept it in the courtyard. I was the one who had wanted it, at any cost. Thanks to a ram, Isaac was spared, because the animal had died in his place. I couldn't understand why Abraham didn't just defy God and try to keep his son anyway. Babo would never have given up a male child, not for all the world, not even if he'd been asked by Allah. He'd have rather turned the knife on his own throat.

During the day, I walked the sheep around like a living trophy, and at night, I hid her in the boiler room so she could sleep indoors. Then, with the adults, we killed her, and afterward skinned and roasted the meat over the embers. No one saw us; we'd done it on a Sunday when the bank was closed. I watched the blood drip onto the asphalt and turn black, the animal's eyes fixed in a lifeless gaze, and thought, *As we live, so shall we die.*

16

Then there were Samir and Aunt Mejra; it was distressing for Uncle Tarik to know they were still in Bosnia.

"We've got to leave; time's running out," he repeated to Babo every day.

"Let's wait till we know where they are. If we leave now, we risk wandering in vain."

My uncle spent the nights smoking in the courtyard behind the house. I could hear him cry, swear, pray, then cry some more. Sometimes my father kept him company, and Uncle Tarik pestered him with his worries. "Did you hear what Fadil said today?"

"Tarik, we need to keep our heads."

"Nadja's son went missing in the escape." My father remained silent. "A three-year-old, do you understand? A three-year-old, and they never found him." Uncle Tarik buried his head in his hands, the cigarette casting a light on his thick hair. "I'm going crazy, Damir. If we don't get any news, I'll go crazy."

Trying to get through to Bosnia was agony. The phone lines in the occupied territories had been cut; to make a call, Grandma had to walk from the village to the free town of Tuzla. She was the hub of all information about our family, hurled and scattered as it was all over the world: Italy, Germany, Austria, America. When she managed to speak with Babo, she was happy, although she could never tell him what we were waiting to hear, where Samir and Aunt Mejra were.

Then one night, out of the blue, she called.

"*Sine*, my son, can you hear me?"

Her voice was tense. My father's heart was in his throat; he feared the worst and was already wondering how to tell his brother.

"They're in Zagreb."

"Mamma, are you sure?"

"I am."

Holding his breath, my father brought the phone to his forehead. He was crying. Grandma was crying too, and after a pause, as if gearing up for a run, she asked him not to forget his sister.

She didn't know that my father, a communist all his life, asked my mother to pray for Aunt Jana every night.

When Babo started working abroad, Granddad asked him to take Uncle Tarik along, and that's what he did. It was common for men to come and go like swallows, bringing home money and prosperity. It had been like this for Granddad, who'd worked as a carpenter in Serbia, and so it was for my father. There was nothing strange about Babo taking Uncle Tarik and leaving his sister Jana and us in Bosnia. Nothing bad can happen to the women, everyone thought.

17

Babo and Uncle Tarik left for Bosnia at night. I woke up and couldn't find them anywhere. My mother was pouring a bucket of water on the stairs. She did that whenever she was worried or frightened or something unexpected happened. *"It brings good luck,"* she'd say. She'd done the same when Babo had told us to leave the village.

"Where are they?"

"They went to get Samir and your aunt," she said, the empty bucket in her hands.

I lost sense of everything around me, the distance to my mother's body, the solidity of the floor under my feet. I couldn't grab hold of the thoughts that were racing through my head and feared they would fly away, one by one. Finally I said, "My head is exploding."

She looked at me, baffled.

"It's all going by so fast."

"What's going by so fast?"

"Things."

She came closer, but my eyes couldn't take in her body. I couldn't tell her what was running through my mind: As soon as I grasped an image, it vanished. Everything was dreadful—what I was seeing, the sensation of not being able to keep up.

"What's wrong, Aida?"

I was afraid I'd frighten her.

"You can tell me anything."

It wasn't true. I could feel that she was sad, and her sadness pervaded my whole being, even my dreams.

She sat down beside me. "They'll come back."

"How do you know?"

She didn't answer. The truth was, she didn't know anything.

18

The next day, I saw Emilia and Franco for the first time. They were walking beside one another as they arrived with the other volunteers. She had short hair, and a light-green jacket was draped over her shoulders. From time to time, she touched his hand, as if to reassure him of her presence. The tenderness of that gesture upset me. I ran inside, gripped by an inner turmoil that I didn't understand and couldn't control.

I heard them introduce themselves to my mother.

"Emilia and Franco," he said. Then the woman asked Mamma how many months pregnant she was.

"I'm due in October."

She touched her belly and my mother let her; actually, Mamma put her own hand on top of the woman's. Next to Emilia, she seemed like a child.

My heart was pounding, and I hid under the bed. Lying on my back in the dim light, I panted like an unbridled horse.

19

We hadn't heard any news of my father for days, and Mamma was anxiously wringing her hands, while I spent every afternoon playing in the courtyard. I jumped in and out of the elastic band, crossed it around my ankles, held it over my head, and threaded my arms through it. I rehearsed these moves over and over, learning them by heart, getting increasingly better and building up precision. I even started doing them with my eyes closed, like a ceremony that required the utmost concentration. The other girls watched me without saying a word. None of them had my persistence; even the best were clumsy, made mistakes, and stumbled.

One day a man approached us, someone we'd never seen before.

"I can give you a bike," he said.

We had some chalk, a ball, and the elastic bands, but the thing we wanted most was a bike.

"I've left it back here. Come take a peek."

We looked at one another. We'd all have to share it, but we'd take turns and set out rules. We checked to see if the woman who was watching us was around. She wasn't. Since no one else had the courage to move, I said, "I'll come."

In no time, I was following him, the others in single file behind me. After turning the corner where the courtyard ended and the street began, we disappeared from sight.

We were holding our trophy high in the air when a swarm of people appeared, shouting and crying. All the women were there—including the one who should have been keeping an eye on us—along with the volunteers, Emilia among them.

My mother, who'd been hanging back, came up to me and grabbed my arm. Emilia was staring at us.

"Don't you dare say a word," she whispered.

She dragged me home and made me lie on the bed on my stomach, and with one hand she pulled down my underwear while she grabbed a mattress beater with the other. She hit my bottom with the handle. I heard it cut through the air before sinking into my flesh. While she was hitting me, she held her belly, as if trying to protect the baby from the smack of the wood.

I didn't want to cry, so I screamed with rage, and two tears rolled down my cheek. I'd been given a beating for both me and my father; he had gone away again, leaving us frightened and alone.

I vowed never to look her in the face again.

20

Two weeks later, Babo returned. Uncle Tarik, Aunt Mejra, and Samir were with him!

I hugged my cousin and smothered him with kisses; his milky smell took me back to our house in the village, to Grandma.

Aunt Mejra took Mamma's hand and drew it to her face. "Forgive me, Fatima. I should have listened to you." Mamma caressed her cheek.

My father and Uncle Tarik looked at each other without a word or a smile passing between them. My uncle left the room, and my aunt followed him, dragging my cousin behind. Babo collapsed in a chair and dropped his head into his hands.

When they'd reached Zagreb, they had been met with chaos. The city was teeming with refugees, and the Croatians packed them into the trains waiting in the stations. Inside a carriage, together with hundreds of others, my father and Uncle Tarik had found Aunt Mejra with Samir, and Aunt Jana too. They could see her bones under her dress, and she stared at them as if she'd seen a ghost.

"My heart was breaking," Babo said. "My sister was right there in front of me, alive, and I couldn't bear the thought of losing her again." He paused. "I wanted to bring her with me, but Tarik said no." They didn't have enough money to buy papers for her as well. At that point, my father had broken down in sobs. In the end he'd given up. He would have liked to leave Mejra and take Jana, but he couldn't bring himself to separate mother and child.

21

Babo and my uncle found stable jobs, and suddenly relationships with the other refugees soured. We continued to share the house with the courtyard, but we were no longer equals. The central issue was how to portion out what we had. Every day, Fadil complained that it wasn't fair to split things among the five families; they needed to be distributed based on the number of children. Babo sympathized, but Fadil pressed on. "You're clever, Damir. You say I'm right, but my three children have to share one piece of meat between them, while your nephew Samir always has one to himself." Fadil was angry with my uncle, with his own wife, who'd had too many children, with the volunteers, with Italy.

One evening we were sitting around a big table set up in the courtyard. It was summer, and the volunteers and our mothers had prepared dinner together.

Emilia came almost daily now. She helped everyone, but we were her favorite family. I watched her from a distance. I longed for her gaze, her hugs, her attention, the small presents she gave me. Yet the most perceptive part of me realized that this would come at a price, so I held back. The warm feelings I had for her were unsettling.

Suddenly Franco asked, "What are you hoping for, here in Italy?"

"That we won't die like dogs," Fadil blurted out.

My father's face turned red. "I expect to be treated like a citizen," he said with clenched fists. "Back home we had everything we wanted. It never crossed our minds to leave; we were kicked out," he explained passionately, and the effort of stringing words together in a language he didn't know very well left him breathless.

Before leaving, Franco approached him. "One of these days, I'd like you and your family to come to our house for dinner."

Babo smiled; I couldn't remember the last time he'd looked that happy. Franco slipped a hand in his pocket and gave me a piece of candy. I waited for my father's nod, then with the speed of a lizard, I hid it away. Franco burst out laughing; I don't know if it was because of the speed or the eagerness of that gesture. It was my candy, and I didn't want to share it with anyone.

22

One evening, Babo wanted just the three of us in our little family to have dinner together. I spent every day in the courtyard in the heat of the August sun, playing with the other children, and at night I felt like I was on fire, as if I had a fever. I struggled to stay awake.

"Come here, Fatima." His voice had a gravity I'd never heard before. I opened my eyes, and Mamma was looking at him too. She put the cloth on the table and sat on the edge of the chair. Her belly was getting in her way.

My father named my mother's cousins, uncles, friends, one after another, finally coming to Hajro, her thirteen-year-old brother.

"They've disappeared," he said, looking into her eyes.

She counted them quietly, one by one on her fingertips. It took some time. Eventually she said, "Fourteen relatives, twenty-two friends." She raised her head to look at Babo, as if waiting for confirmation that the numbers were correct. Then she grabbed hold of the tablecloth. He leaned toward her. They moved gingerly, in silence, as though they were dancing. She suddenly stood up, dragging the chair across the floor, a jarring sound. She went into the bathroom and locked the door.

Babo had been staring at her the whole time. He threw the food, still warm, in the trash. "Go to bed, Aida."

"Where are they?" I whispered.

"Go to bed. You're as white as a sheet."

I was cold, shivering. He hadn't sent me away to keep me from hearing but had let my imagination run wild. I was a child and yet not spared a thing.

The next day, my mother stopped talking. Babo and I wanted to support her, but she chose to exclude us from her grief. Her relatives had disappeared. This simple, unbelievable reality carried her away, until she burrowed into a place we couldn't reach. She wore baggy clothes, mended in spots to suit her changing body, and her hair hung loosely around her shoulders. When I looked at her, I felt scared. It wasn't the thinness of her face or her unkempt appearance; I just couldn't recognize her. And although her features, her eye color, her thin nose, were the same as before, if I observed her closely, I was overcome with a sense of estrangement. Despair did not skin her alive; it caused her to waste away, exhausting her slowly, and left her gasping for breath.

Every so often, my father would say, "Fatima, they've put them in prison somewhere; they'll come back."

He was lying. They had been missing since May, but he feared that her pain would overflow and reach the baby, so he'd waited till summer to tell her.

And as if she knew the truth, she spent all the time gazing blankly at the ceiling, her eyes wide open.

My days were filled with silence, with the stifling heat and boundless river of anguish that dwelled in our little house. I was flooded with the same lethargy that had flooded her. I stayed locked in my room all day, looking out at the treetops, waiting.

23

Babo threw himself into his work like a madman. When he realized that Mamma was struggling to get out of bed, he decided to take her to the hospital. She was seen by several doctors, who all said that she had an iron constitution and that the baby was healthy too. Then she withdrew even further, refusing to push on with life.

Emilia came and looked after her, as you would a small child. She spoke to her softly, resting a hand on hers delicately, as if even squeezing it lightly might break it. Mamma almost never responded. At lunch, when Babo was at work and couldn't find out, she spoon-fed her.

Watching Mamma fall to pieces frightened me, so I spent the days at Aunt Mejra's. But in the evening, the three of us had to sit together around the table, pretending to be a family. My mother forced herself to eat without help, because there was a limit to what my father could bear.

After dinner, I locked myself in my room to cry. I was struggling, and Mamma was too. She took her medications, and every morning, she got dressed and brushed her hair. In those months, we were all her prisoners.

24

My brother was born in October 1992, a skinny, wrinkled baby.

Babo took a picture of him straightaway. "We'll keep this to show to Granddad."

I wondered if Granddad would ever get to know the grandson he had longed for. Every good thing that happened came with a cost: missing those who were not with us and being uncertain of their destiny.

"His name will be Ibro, like my older brother." I looked at him, surprised. Then he added, "He died when he was two. Your grandmother walked to Zvornik to have him treated, but it was no use."

I panicked. What if this baby died too? It wasn't that I loved him, but he'd only just arrived, and I didn't want him to return to wherever he'd come from. Mamma wouldn't be able to bear it. Childbirth had been yet another trauma from which she couldn't recover.

They all must have been worried, because Aunt Mejra came to stay with us. She cleaned and tidied up, chattering to keep Mamma awake. And she wanted Samir and me to always stay nearby; the doctor had said our presence would help her get better.

The baby often cried, but it was as if Mamma couldn't hear him. My cousin and I would peer into the cradle and look at him; he'd stop for a while but would then start up again. He wanted to eat, wanted her body, his cries so loud it seemed he might suffocate.

My father was furious. "Fatima, pick up the baby."

My aunt sat alongside her, placed the baby on Mamma's chest; he squirmed and desperately searched for her nipple through her clothes. That was when I began to love him—unlike Samir, who had felt an attachment to Ibro the minute he'd seen him. He caressed him, took him in his arms; they made each other happy. I stood back and watched them. I was excluded from their joy, caught up in the fear that the baby would go away one day because my mother couldn't take care of him.

25

I spent my days watching the baby. When he raised his head for the first time, Mamma started to speak again. And then we could breathe.

"Don't think about a thing; just get back on your feet," my aunt said to her one day.

"I'm so weak."

"It's normal. We're all weak after giving birth."

She didn't reply. Maybe Mamma was thinking of Grandma Anja and was afraid her child would be taken away, as had happened with Hajro. Or maybe she was missing Grandma and wished she were near.

My aunt went on. "Damir mustn't worry. He's the one who asked me to come here, you know." She paused between one sentence and the next, waiting for a response that wouldn't arrive. "He did that for you . . . He doesn't want you to get tired. And neglect the baby . . . People are talking . . . Anyway, I've told him you're not sick. And you're certainly not crazy."

That word terrified me. I pulled her aside. "What do you mean Mamma's crazy?" I asked with a lump in my throat.

"Darling, your mother is just tired, very tired, and she'll get better with some rest." My mother had always been the more responsible of the two, and now that their roles had reversed, my aunt wanted to take a little revenge. But she saw that she'd gone too far. "And then she'll get back to how she was," she added and gave me a cookie. I refused it, shaking my head no.

"Are you sure?"

"Of course I'm sure."

She never spoke to Mamma that way again, at least not in my presence. She came to help us for months, which was a good thing. Eventually, as she'd said, my mother pulled herself together.

26

One morning, Ibro woke up covered with spots. They were like tiny strawberries, and from the way he was screaming, he must have been very uncomfortable. Emilia appeared out of the blue, as often happened when we needed help. When I heard her coming, I holed up in my room.

She offered to take him to a children's hospital in Milan.

"You'll see. They'll fix him right up, this little one," she said as she wrapped my brother in a blanket and dabbed him with a handkerchief she'd cooled in the freezer. Whenever my mother had to cope with something unexpected, she looked bewildered, but Emilia always knew what to do.

"Aida, we're going out. Go to your aunt's," she said loudly, so that I could hear.

Emilia stopped, with my brother bundled in her arms. "Is she indoors?"

Peeking through the cracked door, I saw her hesitate and resist the urge to come look for me. Mamma pushed her out of the house. "You'll see her later."

Home from the hospital, Ibro was better, and the redness had almost disappeared. I was waiting for Emilia to leave before running to pick him up and hold him in my arms. I'd gotten used to him and loved cradling him when he wasn't squirming. I would watch his lively dark eyes as I plunged my nose into the crook of his neck. His smell gave me such an intense pleasure that I forgot where I was, how we'd all ended up.

I saw Babo and Uncle Tarik running across the courtyard, their faces white with fear. They went straight into the house, and I followed right behind.

Inside, Emilia was washing my brother in a basin, Mamma sitting on the sofa watching them.

"You see, Fatima, you pour the white powder in the warm water, two large spoonfuls are enough, stir it until it dissolves, and then let him soak for about ten minutes."

Ibro was calm, looking at her inquisitively. There was such a sense of intimacy in the room that I felt like an intruder, and maybe Babo did too. Right off, he announced, "Fatima, they've entered the village with tanks."

My mother jumped to her feet, clenching her hands so tightly her knuckles turned white.

"We've got to call," he said.

Emilia stood there, holding my brother afloat as he blissfully gurgled. We exchanged glances; we'd never been so near to one another before. "Call," she said to my father.

"It's expensive."

"Damir, call."

We went to Uncle Tarik's, where there was a telephone. Emilia held the receiver and punched in the numbers of her credit card. "Now you can talk."

My father dialed a number and shut his eyes, praying softly. It was the first time I'd seen him recite the verses of the Koran. We stood motionless, as if one wrong movement might tip our fate. Babo asked a few questions, but mainly he listened. Finally, he handed the receiver back to Emilia.

"Yes, I agree," she said with a slight quiver in her voice.

He looked at her. "One day we'll pay you back."

"It's all right." She put a hand on his shoulder.

Babo lowered his eyes and cried, unable to thank her.

We sat down, and he told us that the soldiers had entered the village and burned everything to the ground. I closed my eyes, trying to imagine our house engulfed in flames, the field where I'd played with Mirko, the granary where Samir and I used to hide whenever we'd misbehaved, my buried dolls.

My father looked at my uncle. "Mamma and Babo ran away to the mountains; they're safe. But some people died."

"Who?"

"I don't know. They couldn't tell me."

Mamma's eyes were vacant; it seemed she could no longer feel anything. Aunt Mejra was gripping Uncle Tarik's hand.

"After the Chetnik troops entered on foot, they sent in the tanks. But our soldiers up on the hill shot their radio link with a bazooka. Their troops got disoriented." He was making sweeping hand gestures and speaking excitedly, as if he'd fired the cannon himself. "Three tanks ended up at the bottom of the valley. The crews in the other two got scared, bailed out of the hatch, and ran off."

Uncle Tarik took the wine and poured out a glass, gulped it down, then followed it with another. Emilia stayed in the background the whole time.

"Their boys are young too; they haven't fought before." My father was addressing my uncle as if it were a matter only for the men. "One of them threw a grenade that accidentally landed in Serbia."

They looked at him to see if he was joking.

"And those idiots said Bosnia was attacking Serbia!" He laughed. And so did Uncle Tarik and Mejra and Samir.

My mother sank further into her chair, sheltering herself with silence and distance. Since she wasn't getting up, Aunt Mejra made the coffee and served a platter of fritters. Emilia wanted to leave us by ourselves, but my aunt insisted that she stay, so she ended up nibbling at her food, like a tiny bird pecking from a bowl. I remember going to sit next to her for the first time, plucking up all my courage to do so. She put her arm around me, and as she moved, I could smell her delicate fragrance. I turned to see if my mother had noticed, but her eyes saw only images of the village, floating and drifting, without a gust of wind to save it from sinking.

As if speaking from the melancholy that had gripped us all, Babo said quietly, "It's as though we are the ones to blame for the war, because we are alive."

27

I grew more attached to Emilia as the days went by. She came to our house, helping my parents in every way possible; our families mixed together like a shuffled deck of cards.

Franco was pleased with my father's devotion to Tito and wanted to hear stories about life in the former Yugoslavia. In return, he gave Babo books on the Resistance and told him about Berlinguer and the golden age of the Italian Communist Party. He even gave him his old party membership card.

"Right-wing people aren't welcome at my table," he repeated whenever we sat down to eat. Babo felt that he was understood, rediscovering the sense of brotherhood he'd grown up with. Franco shared things with him like he would with a son.

Mimì—that's what Emilia had asked me to call her—had started taking me to her house. It was a quiet, well-kept place, with pictures by Lombard painters lining the walls: farmsteads, children in the middle of a barnyard, landscapes that immediately felt familiar. Those images were like an invisible shell, protecting me from all the confusion.

Although I didn't go there often, my escapes to Mimì's pained Samir. I consoled him with the promise of bringing something back, a cake or a toy. After all, he had Aunt Mejra; it was Ibro who was left alone. I kept telling myself that my cousin loved him like a sibling and would take care of him even better than I could. Yet the thought of leaving my brother broke my heart.

My parents didn't seem to notice my absence; they were constantly at the mercy of chaos and never stopped saying that we'd return to Bosnia, that our stay in Italy was only temporary. So when Emilia said they should start thinking about sending me to school, they were taken aback.

"Fatima, do you think she really needs to go?" my father asked one evening at dinner.

"She's doing fine like this; she knows Italian better than we do."

Babo turned to me. "So Aida, what do you think?"

I stared down at my plate, not saying a word. I didn't know what I wanted to do. I'd have gladly gone to school but thought it would be painful for them. My enrollment would be an admission that we were staying in Italy.

My mother was the least enthusiastic about the need for school. She was learning Italian from *The Bold and the Beautiful*; the language was basic, with slow rhythms and repeated words. But there was no way she'd ever be able to pronounce the double consonants or the soft sounds. *La guerra* was "*la guera*" and *quaranta* became "*qvaranta*"; all the bright open Italian vowels dimmed in her mouth. It was as though she brought the darkness of our mountains into the sounds of her speech, which couldn't bend to a different landscape.

One day, without telling me, Babo said to Emilia, "All right, what do we have to do?"

"I've already asked for the application forms. I knew you'd say yes." And she surprised him with a hug.

A few days before I started, Mimì brought me a school bag with a box of pens and pencils, textbooks, and notebooks for writing and drawing. Two large ones had skyscrapers on the cover in vibrant colors with small, illuminated windows. I was thrilled. School would be something all my own.

When my father came home, I showed him the two notebooks; he turned them over in his hands. In the space at the top of the cover, he wrote "DAMIR" in thick, angry black letters.

I found myself holding those notebooks with his name on them instead of mine. I stared at them without understanding, then stuck them into a drawer and made sure never to use them. They'd end up in the trash, untouched.

28

At school, I was a special child. That's what they told my schoolmates, so they were kindhearted and did their best to keep me from falling behind. In the cafeteria, they wouldn't start eating their meat until I was able to correctly pronounce the word *bistecca*.

Every afternoon, Mimì came to pick me up and take me to her house to do my homework. I never heard her ask anyone for permission, and no one complained that I wasn't at home.

Once I was back, I secretly watched my mother making dinner, stealing the occasional glance so our eyes wouldn't have time to meet. I was starting to be embarrassed when I was with her, a feeling that would never leave me and over the years would turn to shame.

At dinner, Babo sometimes burst into a roar, like an earthquake that strikes suddenly, the only warning his impalpable restlessness. His temper paralyzed me; I closed my eyes and ears to shut him out and wanted to disappear into the earth. Ibro stared, motionless, his state of calm so unusual it seemed threatening.

29

The Serbs were constantly trying to occupy our village and drive people out of their homes.

One day, Granddad called my father.

"You've got to get your mother out of here. It's too dangerous; lives are at stake."

He had joined the partisans and was living in the woods above the village but hadn't wanted to bring Grandma with him. "It's a soldier's life. It's no good for her," he said.

My father and Uncle Tarik were on it immediately and managed to put together two million lira to buy her a visa.

Babo had the man who smuggled our packages into Bosnia come to the house. He didn't even give him time to sit down.

"Last time you fucked with me." The man stared at him without flinching. "You kept everything for yourself, and my people over there got nothing." Babo yanked on his jacket. "If it happens this time, I swear I'll come after you. You better watch your back."

My father had an evil look in his eyes that I'd never seen before. He had no choice but to trust that man, and his despair turned him into a different person. The smuggler left with wads of money in a sack.

Over those seemingly endless days, we kept losing hope, only to find it and lose it again.

After two weeks, the man called. "She's stuck at the border. The visa is fake."

My father turned white. I thought he'd start shouting, but he stayed calm. "Where is she now?"

"She's with some fellow countrymen until we can come up with a solution."

I pictured Grandma amid the sea of people trying to cross the border. My father must have had the same thought, because he closed his eyes.

It took him and Uncle Tarik a month to pull together another two million lira.

Babo left on a Sunday morning with a bag full of banknotes, his identification papers and work permit, and apprehension written on his face. Perhaps I had to get used to it; our life would be like this forever, a series of goodbyes without knowing if we'd see each other again.

"I'll be back soon," he said to us before getting in his car.

I held out my hand, looking for my mother's. She stood motionless, her eyes staring straight ahead. Aunt Mejra must have understood because she hurried to pick me up, and I let myself sink into her body.

When there was nothing left to see but the empty street, my mother turned and went into the house. I watched as she floated away like a ghost.

30

"Fatima, don't you have any food for breakfast in this house?" Grandma came out of the kitchen one morning, soon after her arrival, grumbling. It had taken her a few days to pluck up the courage to ask my mother why no one ever touched the pans or went near the stove. No focaccia or bread or potatoes—only coffee and biscotti, like the Italians.

It was the first time Grandma had left the village. Babo told us that she'd kept her eyes fixed on the countryside throughout the journey, amazed at how similar Italy was to her Bosnia.

"How peaceful," she said repeatedly.

We were glad to have her with us, Ibro more than anyone. Samir and I went to school, so before her arrival my brother stayed home all day with my mother, exhausting her. With Grandma, he calmed down. She held him in her arms, told him old stories about the village, about people I'd never heard of, who perhaps had never even existed. While I was forgetting Bosnian, Ibro was absorbing it from her.

Grandma never spoke of the war.

"I don't want to bring here what's happening there," she replied to my father when he pressed her. She didn't like television or spending the day chatting over coffee; she was used to working the land, tending the animals, cleaning and feeding them.

In a small apartment, far from the countryside and the woods, she suffered.

"I really don't know how you can live like this," she said all the time.

Every morning she got up at five, as if she had to let the cows out of the barn. Outside the window, there was only scrubland and the main road that led south, so she sat in a chair awaiting the dawn. Only after sunrise would she make herself a coffee.

"*Nena*, what are you looking at?" I asked her when I woke up.

"I'm looking at my village, at my home."

Samir and I would tease her, thinking her odd remarks were due to her age, or her ignorance.

Ever since she'd started looking after us, we'd become a close-knit family again. Even my parents' mood was lighter. They no longer said they felt old or that they'd lost the desire to live, my mother in particular. She didn't dare say this in front of Grandma; she would have been ashamed.

31

During this time, I stopped going to Emilia's. Not all of a sudden, but little by little, and eventually my visits came to an end. When I was at school, I wanted to be with Grandma and Ibro. Homework failed to interest me, as did the house with the paintings on the walls. My grandmother had stemmed my mother's moodiness and restored the peace.

Emilia came to see us, but we only spoke Bosnian, so she was excluded. She sat back, watching us, and every now and then she smiled, feeling uneasy and out of place.

One day I heard her say, "Fatima, the teachers are worried; Aida is falling behind."

My mother glanced at her and, after a pause, said, "I'll talk to Damir. Thank you." It was clear she wasn't interested, and Emilia looked away.

"Her grandmother watched her come into this world. There's nothing you can do. They're bound by blood," Mamma said coldly. "Anyway, this life is not our life; in a few months we'll go home." A flicker of revenge lit up her eyes.

"Of course, dear. You're right." Emilia took her bag, hugged Grandma, and gave her a smile.

When she moved closer to me to say goodbye, I felt her trembling slightly and looked aside. Her pain weighed on me, but Mamma's eyes were boring a hole in my back. Emilia walked away, her shoulders slumped and a sad smile on her lips. The war was disrupting everyone's lives.

At dinner, my mother told my father what the teachers had said.

"I don't care; we'll be home soon." They spoke in Italian so Grandma wouldn't understand. "The kids are doing much better since she got here," he added, and my mother's back stiffened, her eyes filled with so much anger I was afraid she'd throw her plate at him. Instead, her rage imploded, hiding deep inside her, unvoiced.

32

After a month, Grandma gathered us around the table and said she wanted to return to the village.

"No, Mamma. It's too dangerous," Babo persisted.

She shook her head. "Get things ready for me, you, and your brother." She was adamant. "My husband is there. We've spent our whole life together, and I want to be with him." She couldn't bear to think of Granddad in the middle of grenades, torture, and hunger. "If I stay here, even if he survives, it's as if one of us has died. The war will have separated us."

For Babo, planning her return was as easy as blowing dust off a desk. Within a week, she and Granddad were together again.

We would remain on this side of the border, doomed to our fate as spectators of the catastrophe. The horror we pictured in our minds would dig a trench around each of us.

33

Grandma's departure changed everyone's mood. Every time my father called Granddad, he asked, "Do you want me to come?"

"Why? What on earth would you do? There are two of us here, and we've got a rifle."

Babo seethed with anger whenever he heard his friends had died in combat, and he tortured himself, thinking he wasn't a good patriot. He was in and out of the house, like a raging storm, doing all sorts of jobs to earn money to send home. The more he wore himself out, the more his sense of impotence and frustration grew. Even for us, life was a struggle. And we were hindering his. "If it weren't for you, I'd leave right now."

My mother's only answer was silence.

I responded with biting words, "Never mind; Uncle Tarik can look after us."

"I'd like to see that! The only thing that one can do is drink." Babo had grown hateful, and his hatred spread like oil over whoever was in sight.

My mother had returned to her chair in the corner of the living room, staring off into the distance. Samir and I called it "the Bosnia disease" because we thought she was homesick. In those periods, she forgot to do everything, even to cook. So we turned into two little devils capable of setting fire to the house to bring her back to life. But we only managed to wear her down even further, causing her to grow thinner and more fragile. When she could bear no more of our bedlam, my mother would walk to the balcony railing, raise a foot, and pretend to throw herself off, until we begged her to stop and swore we'd be good. Afterward, we'd hole up at Aunt Mejra's for days.

34

One Sunday afternoon, Emilia and Franco turned up at our house with an apple tart. My mother stood at the door, hesitating, but Babo put an arm around Franco, and in an instant, the gap between the present and the time before Grandma's arrival was bridged.

I was glowing with happiness, although careful to hide it. I had feared I'd lost them and dreaded that what we'd had together was gone. But I was ecstatic, just like the first time. Franco discreetly sought out Emilia's eyes. She touched his arm lovingly, without looking at him. With all my being, I longed to be part of that thing between them that I couldn't name.

Once again, escaping to their house became a regular habit.

"We'll take her to the movies Saturday, and she can spend the night with us. It'll be more convenient," Mimì said to my mother one day. I was seven, and for the first time, I would sleep away from home.

My mother looked at her, baffled, then waved her hand as if to say, *okay, you keep her*. My heart instantly froze. That's what she was nursing, hidden behind her sudden mood swings: her cruelty.

35

On Sunday, my parents came to pick me up and stayed for dinner. It was an evening in mid-November; the Mostar bridge had just been destroyed. I remember Babo standing in front of the television, clutching his head. A final shell from a tank and the arch collapsed, swallowed by the dark water. Then, the desperation of all the refugees. The bridge connected the two banks of the Neretva and united the Bosnian people. We were convinced it was sacred and would last forever.

During the meal, you could feel the tension in the room, like a deep continuous tremor. Ibro added to it. As soon as he was at the table he broke a glass, but then he calmed down once the food arrived. He was struggling with a huge plate of spaghetti and spilling it everywhere. Mimì had pureed some vegetables for him, but my father wanted him to eat what we were eating. "He's only one and already has ten baby teeth," Babo was always boasting.

The television continued to broadcast images of the bridge's destruction. Franco lashed out. "They keep replaying it to persuade us to intervene."

My father held his tongue, his head bent over his plate. Franco grew even more heated and defended Europe's reluctance to use force: it was not their job to stop the Serbs, and definitely not with weapons.

My father let him finish, then said calmly, "Milošević is a vicious snake, and Italy insists on hiding him under its shirt."

It was hard for him to say those words—he cared about Franco and looked up to him like a father—but he had come to a breaking point and could no longer put up with people who failed to understand the situation. Speaking his mind was the only form of resistance he had left.

Franco did not back down; his Russian comrades supported Milošević, so Milošević couldn't be a ferocious, ruthless butcher. "You Bosnians don't want peace," he concluded. "Why can't you accept a divided Bosnia if that's the road to peace?"

Babo smiled bitterly. "You don't understand because you've never set foot in Bosnia." Franco stopped eating. "In Sarajevo, nine out of ten families are mixed. How can you divide them? What do you do with the child of a Serb and a Bosnian?" My father's cheeks glistened. "You can't divide the indivisible."

Even when they'd burned down our house he hadn't cried, but now he was so drained and tired and empty that sadness had finally overwhelmed him.

The dinner went on in silence. Franco couldn't abandon his communist ideals, and my father opposed the breakup with all his might. He wanted the war to end, although that also terrified him. Everything lurking behind whispered words would be revealed; we would meet the survivors, return to our destroyed home.

Babo stood and picked up Ibro. "Get your things; we're going."

Emilia put her fork down. "But we haven't had the ice cream."

Franco touched her hand. "Let them go. It's late."

She looked at me. "Come give me a hug." She came closer and hugged me gently.

I searched for Mamma's eyes. She was waiting at the door, holding my jacket in her hands, looking at me. I was unable to understand what she was feeling; her reactions were mixed with apathy or desperation or want.

Our goodbyes were strange and hurried, as if the ground were burning under our feet.

36

The road was empty and dark. To get home we had to pass fields of growing crops. In the distance, the lights from the houses cast reflections in the fog.

As soon as we were in the car, Ibro got fussy. Usually the car's vibrations put him to sleep, but this time he was having screaming fits.

"Fatima, make him stop."

Mamma reached over from the front and jiggled his car seat, trying to calm him down. He only screamed more loudly.

The car braked in the darkness.

She looked at my father.

"Damir, let's go home."

"Get out." He looked straight ahead; the headlights illuminated the white line separating the two lanes of the road. "Now." His voice thundered inside the car.

"Come on, Aida," Mamma urged as she picked up Ibro. In an instant, we were outside, in the fog.

"Get your bag," my father said to her. Then he put the car into first gear and sped off.

Even after the car's taillights disappeared, we kept staring into the dark.

"He'll come right back," she whispered.

We waited, motionless, my brother curled up in her arms. In the black of the night, space was expanding. I wasn't scared; it felt like I was on a rocket ship. At any moment, we'd lift off and fly away, to a place where all was calm and blissful.

Amid the hushed stillness, my mother began to tremble.

37

"Do you want me to come in?"

"No, you'd better not."

My mother got out of the car holding Ibro, who'd fallen asleep on the way home. She was about to take my hand when she remembered something and turned to Franco. "Thank you. I don't know what I'd do without the two of you."

He smiled. "We'd all be on edge in your situation."

"In your situation" was the magic phrase that made us special.

"Fatima." She turned to look at him again. "Don't make him feel guilty. He's . . ." Franco couldn't find the word. His eyes looked around as if it were suspended in the air. "Exhausted."

My mother didn't respond. That's how the doctors described her state, and yet she was unable to recognize that my father's suffering was the same as her own.

We went into the house. He was waiting for us, sitting on the sofa with his head buried in his hands, all the lights off except a single lamp that cut through the darkness. Standing in the dimness, my mother couldn't help but laugh. And it suddenly came to me. She was saving us again, as she'd done before.

"Help me put the kids to bed." Her voice was soothing.

He raised his eyes; he'd been crying. My mother walked over to him and put a hand on his shoulder. He grimaced, his face full of regret.

"Fatima, I'm so sorry," he whimpered. Just like my brother, he was made of fire.

Mamma stroked his head. "Get up, you crazy Bosnian, and give me a hand." She nodded toward Ibro, sound asleep in her arms.

I looked at them, my mother with a hand on his shoulder, my father searching for her eyes. They too knew how to create that tenderness, as thick as blood, as fragile as a mystery. I loved them fiercely in that moment, a feeling so pure it hurt.

III.

THE SEPARATION

2001/2002

38

Before middle school finished, I had to choose which high school to enroll in.

"I want to study classics at the *liceo*," I came out with at dinner one evening, the day before the registration period closed. I'd waited till the last minute to mention it because I didn't have the courage to tell my father.

"Who put the idea of classics in your head?"

I knew what he meant. "No one," I rushed to say.

"Classical studies are useless," he grumbled. My mother was staring at the potatoes floating in her soup. Ibro was fiddling with a crust of bread. "Do whatever you want. Sooner or later we'll go back to the village."

He'd been repeating that for almost ten years. I lowered my head to hide a smile. One day I would make my own choices, but I didn't tell him that.

Later, Ibro came searching for me in my room. "What's classical studies?"

"It's a type of high school where you study dead languages."

The phrase made him laugh. He was having a difficult time with school, even though he was only in the fourth grade. He was very agile and could run faster and jump higher than his friends, but in class he struggled to control his energy, which always threatened to explode.

And yet his curiosity about the world was as passionate as anyone's, maybe even more than mine.

"I'll do classical studies too."

"Sure. Why not?" I said.

He gaped in amazement. He'd tossed out that statement to test me but didn't expect my response. "Wouldn't it be too hard for me?"

"If I can do it, you can too." His eyes lit up with gratitude; it was impossible not to love his enthusiasm and self-doubt.

"You're such a grind," he said before hugging me and heading off to play in his room.

39

"You're going out like that? You look like a witch." My father was sitting on the couch in front of the television, and a single glance was enough for him to decide that my new haircut was not acceptable.

It was short, just like my classmates wore their hair. The first weeks of school had shocked me. The boys drove motorbikes and seemed to come out of an American TV series; the girls wore miniskirts and low-cut tops that exposed their navels. Babo expected me to behave as if we still lived in our village, even though I was going to school in central Milan. He thought I wanted to reject our roots and distance myself from them. But I only wanted to fit in.

He wasn't prepared for my Italian adolescence, and my every request was met with the Koran. "Religion is more important than you are" was the phrase he used to close down every question, and my mother went along with him. Yet he had always been an atheist; in Bosnia, our house was papered with photos of Tito.

I remember Grandma, in summer, going around in a white camisole and *dimije*, the traditional loose-fitting trousers that clung to her calves, oblivious to anyone's gaze. For the only photo ever taken of her, she had wanted her head uncovered. She had asked my father to take the picture near the forest. "I want the blue sky and the shade from the trees to be in it." He had forced her to smile because she looked so serious, like she was waiting to die. That photo still hangs in our kitchen in Bosnia.

In the village, the women wore western dress; the *šalče* was a peasant custom, not a religious one. They draped it over their heads with natural grace, as if they'd been born knowing that gesture. I watched them so often that my first attempt was as easy as donning a hat, even if I was very young. But when they went to town, they spent the day having their hair dyed and styled, and they teased each other about it being exposed. My mother and Aunt Mejra did the same and giggled like partners in crime.

Here, though, my parents clung to religion as to a higher purpose. They prayed, observed Ramadan, and went to the mosque. But it was not like Bosnia, where we would see the minaret from the house window and hear the call to prayer from the megaphone. Here it was more difficult. And this strengthened their resolve. I had been a good Muslim in Bosnia, then Mimì took me to church, and for a while I thought of getting baptized. I was in such a state of confusion that one day I decided that I was finished with religion; for me, God no longer existed.

My parents' devotion to Allah started with the Peace Accords, when things had settled down and the territory along the Drina became part of the Serbian Republic of Bosnia and Herzegovina—even the forest, our house, the barn. My father was so bewildered that he didn't know how to tell us. The state of Bosnia had suddenly receded, like the water in an outgoing tide, leaving us strangers in the place where we were born.

"This is a Serbian village," the Russian soldiers had said when they entered with the UN peacekeepers. "Muslims can no longer remain here."

The few surviving women gathered outside their houses. My grandma, at the head, had shouted, "Go to the cemetery. If you can find even a single Christian cross, then the village is Serbian."

All the tombstones were Muslim.

The war had ended, the frontier rebuilt, and we'd been cut off from our village. Without even a place to bury our dead.

That was when my parents understood that they had lost everything, absolutely everything, and would be exiles forever, because the country they had known no longer existed. They could only imagine it and dream about it and wish for it, and as happens when return is no longer possible, nostalgia took hold of their hearts. My father turned to anger, Uncle Tarik to wine, while my mother grew overwhelmed by petty everyday worries that drained her of strength.

As for me, I sharpened the feeling of estrangement that I would drag along in my new Italian life.

40

Even if it was only mid-October, the leaves on the trees had changed to yellow from the cold. Babo kept the heat off, so I was forced to study wearing two sweaters. He focused his anger on money. I had to be very careful: he checked sales receipts, the change, everything that passed through my hands.

In the evening, he'd slump on the sofa.

"Here, they walk all over me, they don't pay me enough. This country disgusts me."

He wasn't just angry with Italy or me; he was angry with himself, since he wasn't successful in this second life. In Bosnia, he'd been a brilliant student and, because of his abilities, was given an academic scholarship and became an engineer, then technical director of the steel mill. But all at once, everything had turned upside down.

One afternoon, I had been studying in my room for hours—my fingers and the tip of my nose frozen—with a tenacity that even today amazes me. Suddenly he came in and threw fifty thousand lira on the bed.

"It's yours to spend as you like."

In a week, Ibro would turn nine, and I wanted to give him an Eminem CD. I knew he was crazy about the rapper, and this money seemed to have fallen from the sky. I gave Babo a kiss on the cheek, and he looked at me, confused.

By the next day, I'd hidden my surprise in a drawer. Stretched out on the bed, I smiled, imagining how happy my brother would be, when I heard my mother shouting from the kitchen.

"What's this?" She was clutching a sales receipt. "You spent forty thousand lira on a CD?"

I didn't say a word, and she whipped herself into a crying fit, as if we'd been struck by irreparable disaster. Ibro was standing in the doorway; he knew right away that the CD was for him and ran to hug me. While she was protesting in despair, he was shouting with delight. My father's outbursts and my mother's moods had no effect on Ibro; he refused to let things get under his skin or feel burdened by them. I envied his strength, even if I sensed a hidden vulnerability. At two years old, he'd been capable of banging his head against the wall until he got what he wanted. He'd cover himself in bruises, or faint, or dive onto the floor and hold his breath till he turned blue. My mother would shout and cover her eyes as Samir and I jumped on him, trying to make him stop, but the little devil always scampered off and found a way to injure himself. Frightened, Mamma would agree to everything. "*He's been wild since he was born,*" she'd said time and again.

One of the psychologists in social services had given her a small cane. "Don't be afraid to use it on your son."

My mother wouldn't hear of it; to her, this would be treating him like a dog. So she wandered around the house with that thing in her hand, telling stories about how the teacher at school thrashed her with a similar cane, saying that the heavenly cane had descended from paradise to teach discipline and respect. But she'd never been to school.

41

In Italy, my mother had grown thin.

I realized that when I found an old picture from their wedding. I almost didn't recognize her with those bright eyes and full cheeks. My father has an arm around her waist and she smiles, her mouth slightly open, her head tossed back. She's wearing a veil embroidered with blossoming roses, which she'd rented from a woman in the village, like all the young girls did.

They were married on a January morning, at the end of a heavy snowfall, and had wanted to celebrate outdoors. It must have been muddy and the snow wet, and even though everything looks white in the photos—the forest, the veil, their faces—I'm sure that the dress, dragging on the ground, got dirty.

My mother grew up among her sisters and the fields. Her life should have followed the path her country laid out for women, the things Grandma Anja had taught her. She wasn't even thirty when everything had so suddenly been pulled under and dragged away.

42

Ever since I'd given him the CD, Ibro had locked himself away in his bedroom listening to Eminem at full blast. I was trying to translate some Greek phrases but couldn't find the key to make sense of that mass of words. Exasperated, I stormed into his room to make him turn the music down and caught him dancing barefoot like a madman. He was moving gawkily to the beat, his muscles tense. I couldn't take my eyes off of him. He was playing "The Real Slim Shady," singing and pronouncing every word at a mile a minute, not missing a single syllable. I didn't know where he learned to rap in English like that. It was the same with Bosnian; he knew it better than Samir and I did. When the song ended, he played it all over again. He was wild with excitement, jumping up and down on the bed.

"One day, I'll go to America and be famous just like him and you'll come visit me in my mansion!"

"Get down from there!" I laughed and tried to grab him. "If you break the bed, Babo will kill you!" I hung on to his sturdy legs.

We were clinging to each other when Mamma burst into the room. "Are you crazy?"

The music was turned up so loud that we hadn't heard her come in. She threw herself on my brother to make him get down, but he yanked away and dragged her on top of him. They landed on the bed, holding one another tightly. Ibro clutched her, nuzzling her neck, and she pretended to resist, but that only made him more insistent. He was searching for her body, the same as when he was an infant. My mother was laughing, breathing easily and opening up to us, like on those rare afternoons when we hid in my room and she tried on dresses she didn't have the courage to wear in public, short skirts, and skimpy tops that exposed her cleavage. She clowned around in high heels, strutting back and forth between the bed and the desk, and I could only wish that she would remain carefree and happy like that forever. But those moments were few and far between.

Suddenly, as if she'd remembered something, she smoothed her skirt, wiping away all signs of complicity.

"You silly kids," she said. "You're always getting me into trouble. You can hear the music on the landing. Now the neighbors will tell your father."

Ibro cracked a smile. I could tell he was trying to fix that brief moment of intimacy in his memory, just as I was.

43

I was struggling at school, having to work harder than everyone else because I lacked any solid preparation. The other students intimidated me, seeming totally at ease both in and out of the classroom.

Marta, my desk mate, was my only friend. We studied together at her house, a large apartment in the center of Milan, on the top floor of a building with a view over the trees. I had to explain every lesson to her, because she could never grasp a concept the first time around. It was as if nothing deserved her attention. As a reward, the housekeeper made apple tarts and whipped cream especially for us. At night before closing my eyes, I often thought of Marta, quiet and pale like her all-white house.

For Christmas vacation, I thought we'd return as a family to our village, but my parents went without us, ignoring Ibro's protests.

When they told us we'd be staying with Franco and Emilia, I was secretly overjoyed. Our families had found a way to manage their relationship without allowing themselves to drift apart.

We had a tree and gifts to unwrap after midnight mass. They took us to a movie, and afterward for a cup of hot chocolate.

Every day, Mimì sat with me at the kitchen table, helping with my homework.

One Saturday, despite the cold, the four of us jumped into the car to go to Italy in Miniature. It had been Franco's idea. He took a photo of the Tower of Pisa with us standing underneath, pretending to hold it up. Ibro is shorter than me, and I'm protecting him with my arm. His eyes are lively, his cheeks rosy from the cold, and he's gazing up at me, laughing. I look worried, as if the tower could collapse on him at any moment.

On the trip home, with my brother sleeping next to me, I asked Mimì if one day we could visit all those places.

"But we've just seen them."

"No, the real ones."

"Of course you'll see them, sweetheart."

Our parents would never take us. They only had time, energy, and money for the village.

As if she could read my thoughts, she added, "It's a promise."

Franco cast her a disapproving glance, and she pretended not to notice.

Every now and then, phone calls would arrive from our parents in Bosnia, abrupt intrusions in that large, clean apartment. Babo asked about my homework and said, "Well done, darling. I love you, darling." His tenderness pained me, tempering my happiness. On the contrary, Ibro was excited to hear their voices: he threw himself on the floor and rolled around like an animal. Emilia didn't know what to do; when she approached him, he got even worse.

"You're a rascal," she said in her gentle voice.

Franco wasn't intimidated by his behavior. He was firm with Ibro and showed he could handle him.

44

My parents appeared at the door the day before school resumed. We knew they'd return, but we were still unprepared. I imagined they would carry with them the echoes of a destroyed country; instead Babo hugged Franco warmly, while Mamma smothered us with kisses, holding us tight. Mimì stood and watched, her arms dangling, not knowing where to put them. She wasn't able to hide her shaky voice. With the excuse of going to pack our bags, she escaped into our room.

"Go help her," my mother urged, and we ran to join her.

Ibro asked if he could keep the video games they'd given him.

"Of course; they're yours." She sat on the bed alongside me. "You know you can come over whenever you want."

I looked at her. "Do you let me come here because you want a daughter or because you love me?"

I don't know why I said that. The words popped out of my mouth before I could think. I wanted to be sure she had really chosen *me*, to delve deeply into her kindness even at the risk of hurting her, to soothe the anguish of leaving that home once again and dispel the confusion that had come over me.

Mimì opened her mouth, but no sound emerged. Suddenly, she'd gone blank. She didn't respond to my question, and I never asked again.

45

As soon as we were in the car, my parents became gloomy. By the time we got home it was late. Babo only used low-energy bulbs, and the living room looked cramped and frightening in the dim light. Uncle Tarik came in without knocking, followed by Aunt Mejra, piercing the silence that enveloped us.

"Damir, why didn't you call me?" He was red in the face and had been drinking.

My father walked over to him with open arms. "Calm down." He spoke softly, as if his voice could extinguish his brother's rage.

My uncle backed away; Aunt Mejra was behind him and put a hand on his shoulder.

"She was my mother too." The words stuck in his throat.

Babo rested his forehead against his brother's. Then he settled his gaze on the withering scrubland littering the sides of the road. He let out a long sigh and bowed his head. "Grandma is no longer with us."

I covered my eyes. The pain was so intense that it seemed the crying was coming from someone else. When they turned to look at me, I wanted to disappear. Instead, I screamed. I had seen my grandma in the summer, and she'd kissed us one by one. Her cheeks were wet when she said "*kuća moja mila*," as I counted the wrinkles around her eyes. I hoped that all the electricity in the room would flow through my body and leave me dead on the floor. At least then the desperation that was eating us alive would be released into the air and rise toward the sky.

No one spoke. Ibro hugged me; his eyes were clear and shiny. With my head resting on him, I quietly sobbed, caressed and cradled by his nervous little body. My mother cried silently, as my father gazed down at his hands. My uncle collapsed on the sofa.

Later, Mejra made coffee and fritters, and Samir joined us. Babo was trying to console his brother; he hadn't had the courage to tell him over the phone, although he'd wanted to. He was holding Uncle Tarik's head as he cried.

They recalled the times during the war, when Grandma would leave the village and walk to Tuzla to make a telephone call, two days and thirty miles on foot as the grenades fell. As soon as she was able to get through to my father, she'd immediately ask, "How are you, *sine*?"

"I'm fine, Mamma; you're the one being bombed!" And every time they would laugh.

My aunt was holding my uncle's hand. I looked at my parents, seated apart from one another. They were each fighting their separate battles, not looking for an alliance, just trying to survive.

Babo told us how Grandma had defended our house with a rifle during the assaults on the village. Whenever the Chetniks attacked, she stationed herself in the center of the unprotected house and fired at anyone who tried to enter. Until they managed to plant explosives and blow it up one night. She was the first to see the red brick dust covering everything and our house reduced to a deep, dark chasm in the earth.

46

My brother spent his days at Samir's; I took refuge at Mimì's.

One night, while Mamma was trying to put Ibro to bed and Babo was with Uncle Tarik, I sank into the sofa, thinking back to the day when Mimì took me for a haircut without my parents knowing. We'd paged through a magazine and together chose something that would suit me. Her enthusiasm had dispelled my anxiety.

Suddenly, the image in my mind got blurry and I could no longer see her face. I was afraid of losing her, like I'd lost Grandma and my old life. That would happen one day, despite love and the desire to be close, and the mere thought was enough to make me fall apart. I burst into tears.

"Aida," my mother called in a soft voice.

I looked up; I think she recognized in me the tears of an adult.

She sat down and took my hand. "What is it you miss the most?" she asked, sure that I was thinking of Grandma, of what we'd left behind.

"Mimì," I said quietly. She grew cold and still. "I'm afraid she'll die. Or leave."

My mother didn't know what to say. I rested my head on her lap. She neither caressed me nor pushed me away.

47

By the end of the fall term, I had no grades below average on my report card and some even above. I could now breathe. In February, I started to venture out of the classroom. Marta and I walked through the corridors, looked around, watched people, and made up stories about them, wondering what class they were in, whether they were dating anyone, where they lived.

One day we walked past a pack of guys from junior year. One of them was bragging that his parents had buried his grandfather with the flag of the Padania separatists; the others listened and giggled. He had it in for immigrants. Some of his crew recognized me; there weren't many foreigners in the school.

He too turned to look at me and, retaining his smugness, said, "You're different. You bust your ass to fit in."

His look ripped me to pieces. I could only think of the village and how he would have judged my relatives. To him, I really was no different from the others; this was just his clever way of dodging an awkward situation. Marta stared at me. For the first time, I felt humiliated.

"Don't listen to him; he's a bastard," one of my classmates said loudly, so that everyone could hear. In class, I'd noticed that he usually sat in the last row and didn't talk to anyone. After school, I always saw him with a group of older boys. After supporting me that day, he grabbed me by the arm and pulled me away.

"Look, I know who you are," the guy from junior year shouted at him from a distance. My classmate gave him the finger without even turning around.

"I'm skipping class. Do you want to come with me?"

His eyes were glowing. I'd never met anyone so bold. I could only gaze at him, speechless.

"I know, you're a grind." He smiled.

I kept looking at him until he disappeared behind the door.

That evening, before going to sleep, I imagined myself kissing him, and a thrill coursed through my body. Then my mother's words came back to me: "You'll burn in hell if you go out with an Italian boy." And everything inside me faded away.

One day, as we were leaving school, he came over to me. "Hey, do you want to come to my place and study together?"

I didn't know whether I was happy or frightened. *So this is love,* I thought.

"Sure," I heard myself saying, and I instantly thought of how to lie to my parents.

48

I did it once, twice. For whole weeks, a month. And it was easy. I just said I was going to study with Marta, and that did the trick.

Paolo's house was always available; his parents worked, and the housekeeper came in the morning and left lunch for him to heat up. We shared it between us, then took the dog for a walk. We spent leisurely hours kissing and fondling each other. A tremendous desire blossomed inside me. Sometimes it was painful and I pushed his hand away, only to search for it again.

The rest of the day, I found myself thinking of him constantly, in his room, among his things—the guitar, the sheet music, Bakunin's books—and felt a tenderness for him, as if he were my brother. But he was not my brother; he was something more delightful and more terrible, which stirred me so much that I was no longer able to sleep.

It didn't take Mimì long to put two and two together. When I went to her house to study, I struggled to concentrate.

One afternoon, while I was seated at the table trying to work on an equation, she looked up from her sewing. "I knew it would happen." Then she sighed. "What's he like?"

"He who?" I blurted out defensively. I was embarrassed to talk about him with her, or with anyone for that matter.

"Do your parents know about him?"

"Are you crazy? They'd kill me."

She didn't say another word.

I stared out the window. "He's gorgeous."

"What's important is that he's kind." She smiled at me.

When I went to his house the next day, my pleasure was heightened by the sense of freedom Mimì's smile had given me.

49

We were lying on the sofa, one next to the other, when we heard the key turning in the door. We'd left school after the third period and gone to the park for a walk in the April sun. He held me close, kissed me again and again. I felt the heat from his body deep in my bones. Then the skies opened.

"Let's go to my house. No one's at home."

Once there, we took off our soaked clothes and started throwing them at one another playfully, getting water everywhere. Still freezing, we covered up with whatever we could find. I'd put on one of his mother's tracksuits, when suddenly there she was, in the doorway, with an umbrella in one hand and her keys in the other.

"What are you doing here?" Paolo asked as he sat up on the couch.

"What are *you* doing here?"

She looked at me, and my cheeks turned red-hot. I wanted to melt away. Paolo dispelled everyone's embarrassment by simply putting his arm around me. "This is Aida."

I hid my face in my hands. His mother burst out laughing.

After a pragmatic talk about why we shouldn't miss even a single day of school and then emphasizing that Paolo needed to move to the next grade without failing any subjects, she made us lunch. While she moved casually around the kitchen, she told us she had ducked out of her conference to check on a convalescing patient. She was a surgeon.

"So you've been playing hooky too?" Paolo said. Without looking at him, she swatted the back of his hand with a wooden spoon, leaving behind a smudge of sauce.

A wall of framed photographs caught my eye. There was one of her, in a wedding gown. The photo was taken from behind; she was seated on her own, surrounded by flowers. She had turned her face toward the camera to show off the veil, which fell softly down her back. In fact, it was as though the veil didn't exist—the focus was on the only things that mattered, her and her face. I thought back to my parents' wedding photos, where Mamma was never alone, always with Babo.

Paolo's mother asked me about myself. I briefly told her where I came from. She listened to every single word. "Your parents must be very proud of you."

I nodded, too embarrassed to tell her that they didn't even understand why I'd chosen to focus on classics and that, had it not been for Mimì, I wouldn't have been standing in front of her, in that perfect, shiny kitchen. For Paolo, going to the most prestigious high school was the natural continuation of a path his parents had established long ago, visible in every object that surrounded them. Emilia and Franco's house was beautiful, and yet compared with Paolo's it seemed old-fashioned.

And mine was so different from either of theirs that she couldn't possibly imagine it. Babo had purchased it when it had become impossible to continue living in shared municipal housing. He had gone to the bank and withdrawn a large sum of money, without explaining anything to the teller, who'd rolled his eyes.

"It's mine, and I need it," he'd said.

Even so, it didn't cover the entire amount, and the bank had suggested that he apply for a mortgage. Then Emilia and Franco got involved. "We'll lend you what you need, and you can pay us back little by little."

Babo wasn't sure. He had talked it over with my mother, and she'd cut him short. "Better with them than the bank."

So our families were tied together with money, a knot very difficult to unravel.

One day, he'd loaded us all into the car. We took a back road full of roundabouts, heading south toward the outskirts of the town. Houses grew sparse, fields stretched as far as the eye could see, and eight identical tall buildings appeared in the distance.

"Here we are; this is where we're going to live. Each building is named after a flower, and ours is Rose House," Babo exclaimed. My mother was sitting next to him, unsmiling. Every change upset her, a difficulty that only added to the others. "Tarik and Mejra have bought an apartment here too, smaller than ours."

Ibro started jumping up and down on the back seat; being close to Samir was enough for him. I was in a daze. I would have to leave my friends, I'd be far from school, and from Emilia and Franco. Babo hadn't thought of any of this when he'd made the decision. Even before seeing it, I hated that apartment.

"Where do you live?" Paolo's mother asked me.

And right away, I found myself talking about Franco and Mimì's house.

50

I returned home late that afternoon, still wearing Paolo's mother's tracksuit. My father was sitting on the sofa in the half-light, waiting for me. I couldn't see his face.

"I know you haven't been at Marta's."

I tried to come up with a possible story, but it was too late.

"You've been lying to me all this time." He was staring straight ahead, motionless. He wasn't angry; he looked like an empty sack. I shuddered.

"Babo, I can explain."

"You're not who I thought you were. You've let me down."

I had always thought their warnings about my Italian life were meant to scare me but that once I had a real boyfriend, my father would be more flexible. I felt my eyes swell with tears. "You've let me down too."

He turned and I saw a glare in his eyes.

My shallow breaths filled the room. "You always said that they used religion to divide the Yugoslavian people, that we were all brothers despite our different beliefs."

His lower lip trembled slightly.

"And now you don't want me to mix with other people. Now you put religion first."

I let the tears stream down my face. I don't know how I'd found the courage. I couldn't have said it better if I'd tried.

He turned off the lamp, and in the darkness of the room, I could feel that something inside him was wavering.

Later, sitting on my bed, I wondered where my mother was, if she knew that I'd lied. I listened out for a sound, but none came.

51

From that day on, Babo stopped talking to me, and Mamma was the one who waited up.

Ibro found himself in the crossfire, but for once he wasn't the target. Yet even this new situation didn't make him my father's favorite. Babo was expecting great things from his son, and my brother disappointed him at every turn. Perhaps it was Ibro's way of provoking him, or maybe he just wasn't able to keep up. On the other hand, Ibro enjoyed my mother's unconditional love. She was continually giving him small treats, hiding them from my father. If he didn't like the bread crust, she'd scoop out the soft inside and save it for him.

Aunt Mejra had taken it all in and was worried.

One Sunday afternoon, I saw her whispering to my mother. They were staring at each other, and suddenly, my aunt grabbed her hand. Mamma pulled away from her. "Don't meddle," she said, and my aunt fell silent.

The atmosphere at home was unbearable. I was ashamed to tell Paolo what things were like, afraid he'd think we were weird, or worse, insane. My performance at school dropped sharply. My mother noticed and told my father. There was no way out, and after a sleepless night, I decided to exchange that purported bliss for what I cared about most.

~

Paolo was waiting outside the school and cornered me before I could go in.

"Aida, have I done something to upset you?"

"No."

"So why are you avoiding me?"

I looked away, afraid he might understand. "I've got to study."

He yanked me hard.

"Stop it!" I hissed. My eyes were on fire; he looked down. My heart was being torn apart. "It's because of school. If I don't give it my all, I'll fail."

"What the fuck are you talking about?" I took a step toward the entrance, and he blocked my way. "I promise, if you come to my house, I'll let you study."

We were standing so close to each other that I could smell his hair; he had long bangs that covered his eyes. I had imagined him naked in front of a mirror. A warm sensation spread through my body.

"I miss you," he said.

I wanted to cry. I missed him too; I missed our afternoons listening to music, the jolt I felt in my stomach when he brushed against me. But along with that came everything else: my parents' silence, the words they would use if they knew what we were doing.

He still insisted and a couple of times followed me. I got frightened, and perhaps he did too, because after that he stopped looking for me.

52

With the good weather, the student demonstrations began. In my class, almost everyone went, even Marta. I barely understood what they were about and preferred to stay away. One evening, they appeared on the TV news.

"Is that your school?" my father asked, looking at a banner. Without waiting for an answer, he spouted, "I hope you're not stupid enough to join them."

In Yugoslavia, Babo had been an activist, so I couldn't understand why he didn't want me to be. As if reading my mind, he added, "If something happens and the police come, you risk having your permit taken away and will have to go back to Bosnia and tend the sheep."

None of us had become an Italian citizen. We had to constantly renew our residency permits; the process got more convoluted each time, which was exasperating.

One morning, I didn't go to school and instead joined some of my classmates. We had breakfast in a café and then slowly headed to the meeting place.

"The march never gets started before ten," Marta said.

I was enjoying myself, experiencing a newfound sense of freedom.

As we made our way there, joking around and making lots of noise, Paolo shot past us on his motorbike, with a girl from junior year on the back seat. She was holding on to him from behind, her head resting on his shoulder. We turned to look at them. They were beautiful, their faces radiant.

I put my hand over my mouth and felt the acid from my cappuccino rising in my throat. No one noticed.

"I have to go," I said to Marta and ran off before she could say anything. I wanted to flee to Mimì's, but I'd have had to explain things to her, so I went home, hoping Mamma wouldn't ask too many questions about my sudden illness. When she brought her lips to my forehead, I almost burst into tears.

I spent the whole day in bed. Toward evening, Ibro peeked in with his video games.

"I'll stay with you for a while."

His presence was soothing. I joined the others at the table for dinner. My first bite of food stuck in my throat. "I'll finish in my room."

My parents didn't say a word. I must have looked as if I'd fall to pieces with the first gust of wind.

I hid my plate under the bed and fell asleep, but I woke up in the middle of the night, my heart pounding in my ears, feeling like I was drowning. *I'm dying,* I thought.

I crossed my hands on my chest. The air was all around me; I just needed to let myself breathe. I inhaled deeply and counted to three, several times, until my heart began to beat normally and its pounding no longer filled the silence. I dumped the cold food into the toilet, saw it get sucked down the hole and disappear. In a second, the water turned clear again.

At school, I stopped talking to my classmates. During the break, I reviewed the assignments for the next class. At home, my unwillingness to speak slid into a permanent state of noncommunication.

I kept a distance from everything, as though I had the tender, thin skin of someone healing from a burn.

Ibro was nine and carefree, and at times I lost myself in his joyfulness.

53

During the stressful weeks of final exams, I went to stay at Mimì and Franco's with the excuse of studying there. Even though I'd never said anything, she knew what was wrong and had surely told Franco, because they treated me like I was a convalescent or someone who'd suffered a great fright.

"It's not true that when you're young you suffer less," she told me one early summer evening while we were reading on the balcony, enjoying the warmth of the new season. "On the contrary, everything is more intense because you're unprepared for such a strong feeling of emptiness. You think that love is nothing but hugging and cuddling, and when things change, you suddenly find yourself flung into a disorienting sense of pain. A paralyzing pain, where everything becomes meaningless."

She was speaking of me and also of herself, and maybe of some other child, or of all the children she had desired who had never been born. Since we were unable to talk about these things, we clung to one another as to a life raft.

54

The whole school had gathered around the grades posted on the board.

The line with Paolo's name suddenly jumped out at me. He'd failed two subjects, Latin and math, and would have to retake the exams in the fall. I thought back to his mother's lecture about the importance of moving to the next grade without failing any subjects and tried to imagine what would happen when this news reached his home. Who knows what she'd say to Paolo, or if objects would end up on the floor, in shatters.

In our living room, while I read out my grades, Babo shifted from foot to foot, almost bouncing in place. He did this when he was really happy. I couldn't help but smile.

"Fatima, all B's and three B+'s."

My mother looked at me like you would a prodigy, with awe and wonder.

"Such a brilliant daughter; I'm sure people in the village will be jealous."

I don't think he had any idea what this had cost me.

My father's pride ended quickly; he went back to work, and there were no celebrations.

"It's what's expected of you," he said. "When I bring money home, no one thinks to give me a party or a present. It's what I have to do, and I do it."

All of a sudden, the desolation of summer opened up before my eyes. In August, we'd go to Bosnia. Babo would spend his time rebuilding our house "because it's not like the house will build itself." My mother would be busy with everything else—her in-laws, children, nieces and nephews, the relatives who had managed to survive. Every day she'd prepare food on a gas stove, and on our return to Italy, she would hug her electric oven.

A few weeks after school had ended, Mimì and Franco invited us to dinner. Mamma wore a colorful dress; Babo'd had a shave and a haircut and smelled nice. I felt a slight pang of joy; maybe my report card had brought everyone together and my tremendous effort hadn't been in vain.

While serving dessert Mimì said, as if it were the most natural thing in the world, "Next month, we're leaving for a trip around Italy and would love to take Aida with us. It's our gift for her wonderful achievement."

It felt like the air had been sucked out of the room. Mamma rose to her feet and cleared the dirty plates from the table; Franco understood immediately.

"Sorry, Damir; we didn't mean to offend you," he hastened to say, making it a matter between the men. The help my parents had accepted from Franco and Mimì had given them some economic stability, but now Babo misinterpreted every remark.

Babo lowered his eyes, and a silent stillness followed.

"Can I come too?" Ibro suddenly asked, and his ebullient intrusion made everyone smile. I thought of our trip together to Italy in Miniature; we both deserved this new trip. I drew him closer and gave him a peck on the cheek.

"How disgusting," he said, rubbing his face with his hand. The tension in the room eased a bit, just enough for Franco to add, "If the little one wants to come with us, so much the better." He winked at my brother.

"How long do you think you'll be away?" my father asked.

Franco had played his cards right, and already I was imagining Venice, the Colosseum, the Leaning Tower of Pisa—only this time they would be the real ones.

55

"Do you want us to go up with you?" Franco asked shortly before the car arrived at our building. Mimì looked at him as if it were a given.

"I'll go on my own."

I was afraid to see my parents again. Our trip had lasted a few weeks, and from a distance, their faces, gestures, and words had softened. I wished they could remain just as I'd fixed them in my memory.

"Darling, come over any time to pick up your gifts," Mimì said while giving me a hug. Whenever we visited a city, if I looked at something twice, I'd find it on my pillow before going to sleep.

"To our house," she added.

The keys were in the bottom of the suitcase, so I rang the buzzer; our name was still handwritten and taped on the building directory, as if we were ready to escape at a moment's notice. In the elevator, I felt my heart in my throat.

When the doors opened, they welcomed me with a smile. Babo stroked my cheek; Mamma gave me a hug. "I made lasagna."

I knew she'd have preferred a warm *burek*, some *ćevapčići* or goulash to sop up with bread. She'd made lasagna for me, and that simple gesture filled me with childlike happiness.

"Where's Ibro?"

I was expecting him to suddenly pounce on me. In the end, he'd stayed at home, and his absence had been a faint yet constant torment.

"He's at Samir's; Mejra will bring him here later."

I was a bit disappointed.

I went into my room and didn't recognize it. The desk where I studied was no longer there, in its place a PlayStation console and TV. Clothes were piled on the bed and shoes scattered on the floor. My books, notebooks, and drawings, the photos that filled the shelves, had vanished.

"What the fuck happened here?" My head was on fire with rage.

"Calm down, Aida. Calm down." My father took a step back. "My cousin Emir arrived from Bosnia; he needed work, and I gave him a spot on my team. Since your room was empty, I told him he could stay here."

The frankness of his words disarmed me. They were still the sort of people who slept together on foam mattresses by the stove. I was the strange one, who felt the presence of relatives as an invasion, who, more than anything, longed for a place where I could feel safe.

"Look, we didn't throw anything away; it's all here." My father pointed to some stuff heaped in a corner in Ibro's room. I got closer, and as I recognized my things one by one, I felt like they wanted to get rid of me.

"How am I supposed to study in Ibro's room? Did you think of that?"

"Emir will leave before school starts," my father said with little conviction.

I hoped my brother would get home soon, the only one in the family who would come in peace.

56

At the beginning of August, as soon as my father finished work, we left. He didn't want to lose even a single day, so Mamma and I packed everything ourselves. Aunt Mejra helped us; she, Tarik, and Samir would meet us there a bit later.

Throughout the year, my parents bought clothes, boxes of food, and building materials, which we crammed in the trunk before leaving. Each time it seemed the car wouldn't make it, weighed down by all that stuff, but we traveled to the Balkans without stopping: five hours to Slovenia, two to Croatia, three to Bosnia, three to our village. Thirteen hours straight.

The borders had changed, but not the language. At every crossing we showed our documents, and now, no one asked why we were traveling or where we were going; they knew we were returning to our families. I was careful about the way I looked at the police officers, kept a blank expression and tried not to stare at them. My mother pretended to sleep. Babo got nervous when they asked for our passports and glowered at his face; he felt like a second-class citizen.

To get to our village, we had to cross the Republic of Serbia, the same towns as in the past, but they were no longer part of Bosnia. The Bosnians hadn't returned to their homes yet; some never would.

Every now and then, my father would point one out. "That's where Omer lived. Cousin Ahmed lived there. That one was Fadil's." Until we passed through the village where my mother was born. Then he grew silent, and so did we.

The first deportation took place there, in May 1992. In just one day, seven hundred men disappeared, among them Mamma's thirteen-year-old brother, Hajro. Arkan's Tigers, the Serb Volunteer Guard, had swooped down on the houses, looting and burning them because they believed it was their due. Then they took away all the males, even the young ones.

When they shouted at Grandma Anja to get out, she came to the door holding a coffee grinder because she'd been making herself a coffee. She didn't understand what they wanted, or maybe she wasn't afraid of those men dressed in black, with their faces painted and their bodies loaded with weapons. She'd have even gone back inside to get her clothes had she not seen two soldiers yank her son off the ground and drag him away. She threw herself on him and clutched his denim jacket.

The two men didn't expect her to be so strong. She pulled him close to her, and they tried to pry him from her hands, but Grandma Anja used all her weight to keep hold of him. Hajro was dragged back and forth like a bundle of goods.

One soldier suddenly planted the butt of his rifle between her shoulder blades. Grandma Anja collapsed on the ground. While they shoved Hajro away, she and her son glanced at each other, closed their eyes, and hurled their shouts to the sky. It was the last time Grandma Anja would see him, but she didn't know that at the time. No one knew then that those seven hundred men would be killed. Among them, Mamma's cousins and her beloved Hajro. As soon as it got dark, they moved them to a farmstead in the forest where a twenty-one-year-old soldier was waiting, crouched behind a machine gun.

They faced the wall, ten at a time, hands tied behind their backs; the soldier closed his eyes and fired. He didn't want to see the lifeless bodies fall to the ground, one on top of another. When the pile grew big and was at risk of giving way, a bulldozer hoisted the corpses onto a truck that dumped them into a mass grave. They wouldn't be found for many years; some would never be.

Grandma Anja spent the rest of her life preparing to return to her house. She bought plates, cups, and sheets and packed everything up so she could put the new things back in place, where the old had once belonged. She died thirteen years after the war ended, when strangers still slept in her bed. She had chosen the exact spot on the hill where she wanted to be buried.

"You can see my house from here," she'd said. "And when you find my son, I want you to bury him next to me."

While the funeral procession walked up the hill, the Serbs stood at the windows of her house, keeping their eyes on the coffin until it was finally covered with earth.

A few days before Grandma Anja died, my mother had asked, "How has life turned out for you?"

"It went by in an instant, in the blink of an eye. It was over just like that." And she blew softly, as if snuffing out an invisible candle.

Grandma Anja died in good health. She'd even gotten some new teeth. What killed her was the war, and the black hole left by Hajro's disappearance. As an old woman, she often recalled the day she had clutched his denim jacket, and her wrinkled cheeks would become shiny with tears.

"I can still hear him shouting as he slipped out of my hands." And she'd look at her hands, as if she might find him there.

My mother never told her the truth, not even at the end.

57

We were making our way through the woods; at every turn, I expected to see the valley open up and the first rooftops emerge. I watched my brother; Ibro was born in Italy, and for him the village was just a place evoked by the adults' stories. Yet our house belonged to him, even before its construction was finished.

When we reached the village, the few remaining children surrounded our car, giving us a hearty welcome. My father pulled money from his pockets and handed it out; perhaps he felt like the Prophet or Jesus or one of the apostles.

I was embarrassed by the looks the people gave us. We had a big car, nice clothes, new shoes, and lots of games. In their eyes, we were "the ones who returned but didn't stay," no longer a full-fledged part of the community.

Only Ibro felt at ease wherever he was. He got out of the car and immediately walked off with the group of children. In Italy, he met the other kids in the square, on the playground, at the football field and the church youth center, like any other Italian boy. In Bosnia, he was a child of the village; he spoke the language, romped around with the animals and the other kids. Six years younger and perhaps I too wouldn't have felt out of place wherever I was.

Granddad came to meet us, his hand on his heart. Mamma pushed me toward him, so that I could give him a hug.

"Go on, Aida."

We found ourselves embracing, but our bodies lacked intimacy. My grandfather had never held me warmly. He'd always had a soft spot for Ibro—the youngest male in the family—even long before he was born. And I was angry because I thought he didn't care about me. But after I'd enrolled in high school, he'd started asking about me and wanted to hear about my studies. Then Ibro got the sweet-talk all to himself and I the intelligent chats and smart advice.

While he helped us unload the car, even before we set foot in the house, he started listing for Babo all the relatives who'd sent their kids to school.

"Those parents are the richest in the world." Then he turned toward me, but made sure Babo would hear, and said, "Now your father must save money, sell the house if he needs, because you will go to university."

My mother, standing in the doorway, smiled, her bright eyes caressing me.

"*Najpametnija*," she said. "The most wise one."

If she had looked at me like that every day, I'd have been hers forever.

58

The August days commenced, each one identical to the last. In the mornings, I helped Mamma around the house, and in the afternoons I did my homework and had some time to myself. We lived on the ground floor and in the basement, which were more or less finished. My father and four other men were working on the first floor, trying to bring water from the well into the house.

"I want to put in a swimming pool," I heard him say during their breaks. The other men laughed. Babo was stubborn. He wanted to build a house fit for a big city, instead of a remote village on the Drina, where we'd gotten electricity only because he'd dug in his heels. He'd physically carried the equipment to the house with five other men. They'd planted the pylons and strung the wire for over two miles, and still, he'd had to pay for the installation.

"Your father puts everyone else before us," Mamma whispered with veiled resentment when he was out of earshot.

Even Granddad tried to discourage him. "People don't like to feel obligated; they'll be envious and will hate you."

Babo didn't give a damn. He liked showing off and enjoyed the prestige he had in the community.

He was so convinced about the pool that he called in three other men to help. At first, my mother cooked for everyone. Then one night she confronted him without even waiting for Ibro and me to go to bed.

"It's okay to build this swimming pool that no one needs, and it's okay to pay these men to help you, but I'm not going to cook for everyone."

I'd never seen her speak to Babo so directly. He looked up from his newspaper with his mouth open, like a bird waiting for food. I expected him to explode. Instead, he didn't say a word. Mamma finished drying the plates and went to bed. Babo followed behind, meekly. That scene made me happy; she too, then, was able to assert herself. I vowed to always remember it.

59

The evening our aunt and uncle arrived, Ibro was more excited than usual. He'd been waiting for Samir for days. Babo too was happy to see his brother there, as if they were both reattached to their roots. Mamma had prepared the most traditional Bosnian dishes, and when my aunt saw them on the table, she gave her a big hug.

They took off their shoes, and we sat down together, Granddad between Babo and Uncle Tarik. They looked at the photo of Grandma hanging on the wall. They prayed.

After dinner, Granddad took out a deck of cards. Mamma and Aunt Mejra went off to wash the dishes. Their figures moved nimbly against the light: my mother thin and nervous, Aunt Mejra less slender and with a hint of indolence. Samir and Ibro took refuge in their secret games. As we played, we stopped talking. Uncle Tarik drank and smoked. When it was his turn, he drew a card.

"No," he shouted, putting his hand on his forehead. Babo laughed.

They were so different. My father called him his restless, vulnerable brother. Ibro and I weren't at all alike either. When something unexpected happened, my body turned as cold as ice, while he gave off enough heat for the two of us.

As I looked at my cards, I heard my mother telling my aunt about our neighbor Amela, who'd come to visit us that morning. She was just a few years older, and when we were little we were mistaken for sisters.

She'd shown up with her husband and baby. A beautiful chubby little girl, she told my aunt, giving me a disappointed look.

"Aida isn't like us," my aunt remarked. "She's meant for a different life."

My mother brusquely took off her apron. "I'm going to hang out the laundry." And she walked out of the room, letting in a gust of cold air.

My aunt's eyes met mine, and her gaze went blank for a moment. Before going to bed, she joined me in my room. She wanted to see my textbooks, even the Greek ones.

"You must be a real genius to understand all this stuff!"

She gave me a pinch on the butt, then another. I was trying to put up a fight, laughing. She was laughing too. She took the scarf from around my shoulders and tried to cover my head. I took it off and, in an instant, arranged it on hers. My hands still knew how to do it.

"I haven't worn this in donkey's years," she said, looking at herself in the mirror. "Tomorrow you've got to take a picture. I don't have any of me in a *šalče*."

She hugged me and showered me with kisses.

60

Time moved slowly, a cradle that swaddled and comforted me. Even my parents' rules on clothing, schedules, and prayers at the mosque were less rigid, as if just being in the village were a guarantee of good behavior.

"Don't you like any of the boys here?"

I was washing the dishes, and the question hit me like a sharp stone. "No, and I never will."

"You can't know that."

She failed to see that I had nothing in common with the boys in the village. I wasn't confident speaking the language; my Bosnian had gotten fuzzy. After the war, any words that sounded Serbian were seen as provocative. When I was a child, I used to say *dov-idjenja* for goodbye, but now it sounded a bit Serbian, so I chose to smile rather than speak. These days everyone in the village said *selam aleijkum*. My father refused to respond with *aleijkum selam* and constantly risked getting into an argument.

"I don't want to use the language to take sides," he said.

In the evening he'd bicker with the former partisans, those who had survived. After all the bloodshed, the men who'd stayed in the village didn't trust their Serbian neighbors. They said hello in passing but would never have coffee together in one another's houses. Babo would get heated; he thought it was foolish to hold a grudge against the Serbs. Sure, after the war the Bosnian state had been divided among Muslims, Serbs, and Croats. But for seventy years they'd lived together, spoken the same language, eaten from the same plate. They'd only differed in religion. The Serbs were our neighbors, and we'd always helped each other, even in the most difficult times. We donated blood if it was needed. My father's best friend was a Serb he'd gone to school with; he was more than a brother to Babo, who still loved and respected him and kissed him when they met. At the beginning, when they'd kicked us out of our homes and turned them over to the Serbs, many refused to enter and were killed, just like our people.

Uncle Tarik shook his head, while Aunt Mejra counted his empty glasses and scowled at him. He told Babo he was wrong, that the Serbs hated us. He reminded him of a few certain people who'd been betrayed by the neighbors and shot dead in broad daylight, after being forced to drop their pants to check if they'd been circumcised. Because they wanted Muslims to die like dogs in front of everyone, their faces on the ground and their asses in the air, without a shred of dignity.

My father raised his voice. The ethnic issue was just bullshit, an excuse to tear Bosnia to pieces and divvy it up. Uncle Tarik got furious and went on a rant, shouting that the Serbs wanted to eradicate the Bosnian state because Bosnians were Muslims. Babo stormed out, slamming the door, his heavy steps circling the house as he smoked half a pack of cigarettes. I can still see that intermittent glow as he sucked them down to the butt. He couldn't accept that Bosnians and Serbs hated each other—it was too painful—and he couldn't accept that his brother didn't see things the way he did.

Granddad tried to restore the peace. He made Babo and Uncle Tarik sit next to each other and spoke to them with patience. Even for him, it was no longer the same, but you had to forgive, and never forget.

Granddad had fought as a partisan; he'd survived eating bark off the trees, running through bullets that spewed like lava, to defend the village and their homes. So Babo and Uncle Tarik kept quiet. Out of respect, not conviction.

61

One morning I woke up and Babo was already dressed, wearing his favorite shirt.

"Where are you going?"

"To Grandma's grave."

I looked down. "Will you wait for me?" I'd found a way to avoid going on my own. He nodded. I was about to put on sandals, but he handed me a pair of boots. "It rained hard last night."

I imagined the rain washing the forest and the gardens, intensifying the colors. We walked apart, through the alleys of the village, that "sprinkle of houses" we'd always called it. Babo looked at the dwellings across the fields, in the Serbian Republic. I was sure he knew every person, every tree branch. I knew he suffered from the separation; those places belonged to him regardless of any treaty, convention, or political decision.

We followed an unpaved path, our feet sinking into the mud, along a barbed wire fence that was impossible to grab hold of. I moved slowly, Babo quickly. Every now and then he slipped, landing on his backside, and we burst out laughing.

At the end of the path I looked around. "I thought Grandma was here."

"We have to turn left and climb another hill."

Once we were on the new path, we came across a soldier with a rifle slung over his shoulder. Babo said something to him; I deliberately didn't listen. I didn't want to know what he was doing out there dressed like that or why he needed the rifle. I saw the house where our neighbor Amela lived and thought back to her visit; she'd let herself go a bit, and her baby was fat, but she seemed happy. Truly happy.

We continued walking up the valley; the sun was high, and our shirts were stained with sweat. The moles had made holes everywhere, and Grandma was buried among them. I let Babo go first.

I saw a mound of earth on the ground. Grandma's body had not yet had a proper burial.

Babo raised his open hands to his chest. I did the same and whispered a prayer, the first my mother had taught me when we arrived in Italy and the only one I remembered. I never knew what it meant and hoped it was the correct prayer for the dead. I didn't want my father to notice that I didn't know how to pray.

When he finished and turned to me, my face was wet with tears. We were both overcome with embarrassment. In the stifling heat, he took my hand and brought it to his cheek. It was damp, like mine. We sat close together, without speaking. I had the impression that the silence resounded from one hill to the next. I enjoyed the silence of the valleys, and of the people.

"Granddad wants that plot for himself." He pointed to a space next to Grandma. In that instant, I knew it would be different for us, that we would not be buried together on those slopes. I looked at my father; maybe he realized it too.

Next to them was the tombstone for Granddad's twin brother, whom I never knew. He'd died young, in a fire that destroyed his house. Some people said he'd started it on purpose because he was unhinged and wanted to end his life.

There was an Arabic inscription engraved on the stone. I pointed to it. "What does it mean?"

"I don't know." He looked more closely. "Maybe *mehraba*, 'may peace be with you.'"

I knew that word; you use it when you meet someone for the first time. I've never found an expression more powerful. It's the most beautiful thing you can say to someone: "May you live in peace."

As we walked back down, he showed me where his cousin Ibrahim was buried; he'd been killed by the Chetniks in 1992. That year weighed heavily on me. In place of the stone marker, his grave had a block of wood painted in green with the names of his three children written in white.

I looked at my father standing there and wondered what would have happened if my mother and I hadn't managed to find him and cross the border. Maybe I wouldn't have been constantly torn between two places and would now be resting on the hill with all the others.

In a heartbeat, we were on the tarmac road, surrounded by fields of growing crops. The farmers had already bundled the wheat, and the sheaves of *žito* were arranged in neat rows. As a child I'd collected them with the other girls, under the blazing sun. The men told us we weren't good at it and showed us how to rake them up. We got terrible headaches, our calves were covered in cuts, and our backs ached. During the breaks, we swore at the Serbs beyond the hills, as if they could hear us. Before going home, we washed off with the icy water from the well, and in the evening, the food tasted better than ever. Our mothers had smiles on their faces because they hadn't seen us all day.

I wished I could rake up my days like I'd done with the *žito*, make them smooth and orderly, without any unexpected rough bits.

62

I heard my mother coming down the basement stairs, short of breath.

"Aida, spruce yourself up," she said just as she saw me. I had on a pair of sweatpants and a tank top. I gave her a puzzled look but didn't move from the book resting on my knees. "You have a visitor."

I couldn't think of a soul who might be looking for me there.

"It's Mirko," she said, and a vivid image flashed before me of him at the age of six, running away with the fear of war on his shoulders and a sensitive look in his eyes as he tried not to hurt me. I hadn't seen him since. My anxiety was growing as the seconds passed. I pulled my hair out of a ponytail while my mother went ahead of me up the stairs. I tried in vain to imagine Mirko's face on a sixteen-year-old body.

A moment later, I saw him standing next to my father, near the front door. He was tall and thin, with acne on his cheeks.

"Offer him a seat, Damir," my mother said as soon as we entered the room. "Would you like a coffee?" She went to the kitchen without waiting for a reply.

Mirko and my father sat on the sofa. I ducked out with the excuse of helping her.

"What are you doing in here?" my mother asked when she saw me.

"I don't know what to do in there."

"Let him do the talking. He came to see you, so he's bound to have something to say."

It was good advice. We went back to the living room; she took in the tray with the coffee, orange juice, and cookies, and I carried a stack of paper napkins. I sat next to my father, and my mother next to Mirko so she could observe him without being noticed.

He was talking about his family. They had escaped to Tuzla, where they stayed for the whole of the war. Later, his parents went to work in Germany, together with Mirko's brothers. He'd refused to leave Bosnia to join them. In the end, they entrusted him to an aunt who'd lost her children. He was in high school and wanted to go to college to become an engineer so he could work in the country. My father's gaze revealed his admiration for Mirko, a young Bosnian who wanted to rebuild our homeland, all that I, and perhaps even Ibro, would never be. My father threw me excited glances, unable to understand that I didn't share his enthusiasm.

Mirko's presence, like his story, left me indifferent. I no longer saw in him the child I'd once loved, his sudden explosive laughter, his clever, easygoing way of treating adults. Now his faint smile wore a meekness I didn't remember.

"Why did you come all this way back to the village?" my father asked, since he hadn't mentioned it.

"Because of our house. My parents want to sell it, and I'd like to fix it up." As he said this, he looked at me. "I thought I'd do it over the summer, during my school vacation."

"And we'll help you!"

"I'd also like to come see Aida, while you're here." My eyes must have popped out of my head because he quickly added, "If it's okay with you."

It was the first time he'd spoken to me since we'd sat down.

"Come whenever you'd like," my father interjected and turned to me, beaming. My mother could hardly contain her joy.

Mirko said goodbye to my parents; at the door, he shook my hand and promised, "I'll see you soon."

It was all too baffling; I couldn't respond, only look away. As soon as he left, I ran down the stairs, locked myself in the basement, and cried with rage.

63

We didn't talk about Mirko again until he showed up at our house, five days later. My mother brought him down to the basement. I said hi and went right back to translating a Latin text, pretending all the while that he wasn't there. He didn't utter a word. In the end, he said goodbye and left. That night I went to bed without any worries, having easily shattered all his expectations.

He returned the next afternoon at the same time. When I saw him at the door, I could barely hide my surprise. He sat down in the same place, took a crumpled book out of his jeans pocket, read until I finished my Greek translation, then got up and left.

The scene repeated itself for three days. On the fourth, exasperated, I spoke out.

"Why are you here?" My voice bounced off the walls in the bare room.

"Because I want to get to know you." A simple answer. "You and I were like this." He linked his right finger with his left one. Then he added, "Before."

Our whole life was divided between a before and an after, regardless of how old we were—twenty, fifteen, or eighty. Life before the war existed in a parallel dimension, and at times I wondered if it had ever even existed. The answer was there in front of me, in flesh and blood.

"I'm not that little girl anymore."

"That's why I want to get to know you."

He stood up. I thought he'd come closer, but he walked away.

I didn't sleep that night. If I couldn't discourage him, I had only one option left.

When he turned up again, I was prepared. "Let's go out."

He was surprised but didn't show it. We walked along the plowed fields in the crushing heat and found shelter in the shade of a massive bundle of prickly *žito*. He took the cigarettes from his pocket and handed me the open pack. In the village, the women don't smoke; it's as vulgar as spitting. If a woman really wants to smoke, it's best done in secret. He was offering me a cigarette in broad daylight. I refused, but his gesture had bridged a gap. His boldness was intact. I smiled.

He told me how it had been painful, but exhilarating, to be uprooted. In Tuzla, he'd witnessed the river of refugees fleeing in every direction.

"Faces, the faces of thousands of women and children." His eyes grew wide. "Children our age getting lost in the chaos and disappearing."

I could envision that hell on earth, an exodus in the sweltering heat and freezing cold of Bosnia, people carrying all they could from their homes, and these new images overlapped with those I had from the border at Sežana.

He talked about the bombings and the hunger, about his parents having to sell everything for a few ounces of sugar because he and his brothers hadn't eaten in days, about the dogs howling in the night that suddenly grew quiet because someone had eaten them.

As I'd always done, I listened. There was nothing to say; I wasn't there when the worst had happened. I'd been told that the Chetniks had been firing shots in the vicinity of our house for forty days before we escaped, and I didn't remember a thing. I didn't see my garden in bloom or our house explode. I didn't see my dolls unearthed; I didn't see them burn. All I could remember was a river and my grandmother's fairy tales.

So I kept silent as Mirko told me where he was when the grenades fell near his house, while in the streets people were dying. The ones who'd stayed behind had found a purpose; I had found the silence of those who'd fled and now no longer knew where they belonged.

"You see, I want this place to go back to how it was. I'm not interested in moving to Germany to work as a slave, like my brothers. If I have to break my back, I'd rather do it here, where I was born."

As I listened, his words released the opposite desire in me, and for the first time I was able to express it clearly: He wanted to stay; I wanted to leave.

In the lull, he pulled a box of Bananicas from his backpack. I couldn't contain my joy. "Where on earth did you find them?"

"In Tuzla. They're not the same as the ones we liked, but close enough."

They were disgusting, banana marshmallows covered in a layer of chocolate. But they were the candies of our past.

I let him grab the first one. Every bite rekindled a piece of our childhood. That day, we gained our innocence for a second time.

"See, everything's still the same." He pulled me to him. Maybe it was the heat, the thoughts piling up in my head, or the cloying taste of the Bananicas, but I let him. He gave me a long, gentle kiss.

I backed away. "Let's go."

He followed behind without speaking. We stopped just outside the village.

"That was lovely, but don't come to see me again."

He gaped, as if to ask why, but I beat him to it.

"There's nothing more to say."

I stroked his cheek and ran off, without looking back.

That night my sleep was restless, filled with visiting ghosts. I woke up, and in the stillness teeming with wild distant sounds, I felt the warmth of his lips, the energy of his body, the strength radiating from his conviction. I hadn't only kissed him, I had kissed my buried ancestors, the dead torn away by the war, the life I could have had and no longer wanted.

In the morning, my mother greeted me at the kitchen door.

"I made a little cake, so when Mirko comes you can have it downstairs."

"Mirko isn't coming anymore."

She looked at me as if she'd seen something frightful. "What's gotten into you? Are you cursed?"

Yes, maybe I was cursed, maybe all sorts of curses had been cast on me. All of them coming from that land.

64

We returned to Italy. School resumed, and it was as if life were beginning again for me. Studying was my refuge. I committed to working harder than the previous year, closing myself off from everyone, even Ibro. I watched him from afar and felt slightly nostalgic.

He retained his exuberant energy; time wasn't making him any more thoughtful or measured—the shock-emitting hurricane carried on. My mother left him to fend for himself, using as an excuse her now rare ailments, which left her exhausted and weak. On occasion, my father would explode in a rage, but to no effect.

At the end of October, Cousin Emir was still living with us and showed no signs of leaving.

I began spending time at Mimi's again, going home only on the weekends. I waited desperately to be with her, but when the moment came, I was beset with an acute grief. I felt separate from my family, and the separation was slowly digging an invisible hole, while in that hole another part of me—small, blind, vulnerable—was growing. But growing was painful; separating was painful. I fantasized that my parents would suddenly be struck dead and I'd be free. Then I felt guilty—what sort of person could have those thoughts? I was wicked, and maybe my father's anger and my mother's unhappiness were my fault. I watched how Aunt Mejra laughed with Samir, how she squeezed his face and hugged him tightly. I too wanted to lose myself in that raw happiness that comes from the heart. In those moments, I threw myself on my mother and pressed my face hard against her belly. I thought she knew everything about me, even the mean thoughts that I was ashamed of. Leaning into her, I tried to make her forget, and I sobbed. If she could forget, she would love me more.

She remained motionless, wetted by my tears, because there was nothing more she could do.

65

One Saturday in November, we were sitting around the table. Mamma had ordered pizzas; she almost never felt like cooking. I remember that autumn as long and damp, without even a day of sunshine to brighten the sky.

While we were waiting, my father looked down and said point-blank, as if it were the end of a conversation we'd previously had, "You decide where you want to live—with them or with us."

I could feel every single word hit the ground and splinter. And a great cold spread through my body, so sudden that in an instant it froze all my tears.

I went to my room and, under Ibro's watchful eyes, filled a suitcase with the things I didn't want to leave behind.

"Aren't you coming back?" he asked.

I looked at him; he would be there alone. *He's just a child,* I told myself. *But he's strong; he can handle it.*

At the door, I put on my jacket. Mamma came out of the kitchen with her apron tied around her waist. She kissed me on the cheek.

Ask me to stay, my broken heart demanded. But she didn't, and neither did my father.

So the matter was settled.

IV.

THE RETURN

2012/2013

66

At first, he threw it back in my face. "That night, you didn't even say goodbye."

"When?"

"When you left us for your other life."

"Yes, I did, Ibro," I tried to rebut, failing to believe it myself. I had no memory of saying goodbye, only of thinking that I was leaving him there. I was so tired and confused that I'd behaved like a coward.

I don't even know if there had been an arrangement between our families, whether a decision had been made or things just tacitly accepted. In that murky situation, each of us had something to gain and no one had the strength to set any boundaries. I had devoured all the opportunities that Emilia and Franco could offer me: trips abroad, a new car when I turned eighteen, permission to smoke. I wanted the prestige that comes with being a doctor and at last had earned a degree in medicine with top marks.

My father was convinced that I'd sold out, although he didn't have the courage to say so, and I'd stopped talking to him. Contact was limited to sporadic phone calls with my mother, to make sure they were still alive and well. Only the thought of my brother continued to gnaw at me.

At twenty-three, I had asked Emilia and Franco to adopt me and took their Italian last name. I signed all the paperwork quickly, hardly glancing at it. I'd be Emilia and Franco's sole heir. From the outset, so many of my choices had been intertwined with money, and it would have been useless to try to pretend otherwise. By this point, I felt that I was entitled to compensation for what life had thrown my way, and no matter where it came from, I was ready to take it without a shred of guilt.

Franco had insisted that I invite my parents to my graduation day.

"You'll be sorry if you don't ask them to come."

"I don't think so."

"Do it for Emilia."

I knew my father felt robbed of a daughter, and he blamed her. She'd gone from being a savior to a thief. Franco had been trying to repair the rift, and perhaps he saw my graduation as a good occasion to gather us around the table, like in earlier days.

We were standing outside the restaurant—a couple of fellow students, some of Franco's relatives, friends of Emilia's who regularly came to the house. I was ecstatic. I was a doctor, what I'd worked so hard to become. Then I saw them in the distance. My father was wearing a jacket, which he buttoned up just as he got out of the car. He was bouncing in place. My mother was clutching a handkerchief; she either had been crying or was about to. They were alone.

I immediately asked, "Where's Ibro?"

My father's reply was curt. "Better if he doesn't come." My mother touched his arm, but he was unfazed. I continued toward the restaurant. I wasn't going to let him ruin my happiness.

Ever since my brother had dropped out of school in his final year, my father was always on his case, and Ibro had become even more unstable and quarrelsome. Sometimes Mamma cried on the phone, and I attributed the tears to her tendency to overreact. Ibro and I regularly met in secret, and nothing seemed off with him, apart from his usual exuberance. He was obsessed with the passage of time and felt he had to do something important right away, make money right away, become famous right away. He got angry with my father because he refused to sell the house in Bosnia and free up funds for him to make a hip-hop album. He wouldn't hear of going back to school. First he wanted to be a cartoonist, then play the saxophone—but he could never finish what he started.

When I was about to give up hope and celebrate my graduation without him, he turned up with a bunch of gigantic lilies covering his face. His impulsive gestures moved me, but I didn't want to cry. "You're such a nutjob! How much did they cost?"

I hugged him. He was drenched in perfume.

"Come on, Aida, let's go in."

I wanted him to sit next to me. He clowned around the whole time, dissolving the tension into an atmosphere of relaxed joy.

A cousin of Emilia's asked me, "What will you do next?"

"Anesthesiology and resuscitation."

Amid all the congratulations, Franco asked my father, "Damir, are you pleased?"

He didn't answer, and a strange silence followed.

"Of course, we're very pleased," Mamma said.

My father looked at me. "I'd have preferred for her to study surgery. What should I say in Bosnia? That my daughter puts people under so the surgeon can operate on them?"

He hadn't lost his ability to deliver a sudden blow.

Ibro started tapping the table. "Let's drink a toast to Aida!"

I don't know whether he refused to understand or he'd become impervious to my father's hostility. He challenged him openly, without fear. Or at least that's how I saw things.

Then everything turned upside down.

67

He'd just returned from London, his first trip on a plane, a present my parents had given him for the Feast of Sacrifice. That year, it fell at the end of October, near his birthday. He was turning twenty. He'd gone to London with some friends, nice guys whom I knew. *Nothing bad can happen,* I thought. *At most they'll smoke a few joints.* He'd landed at Malpensa in the afternoon, and in the evening had gone out for a walk in the neighborhood. At six the next morning, he still hadn't come home.

At the sound of the intercom, my mother got up. The room was pitch black. My father stayed in bed, awake, in unspoken disapproval.

"Hello?"

"It's me."

Mamma recognized his voice, opened the door, and went back to bed.

"What time is it?" my father asked from under the covers. He knew but wanted to hear it from her.

"Ten past six."

"That's great," he quipped. A second buzz from the intercom broke the silence. My father grumbled; my mother jumped back up.

"Yes?"

No answer, so she put on her sweats and went to see what was happening, neither of them saying a word to the other.

When she saw Ibro, he was a different person, his gaze so transfigured that it made him unrecognizable. I still remember the anguish in my mother's voice when she told me.

"Ibro, come in the house."

He was chuckling, in short uneven bursts. "Mamma, I've found love."

Surprised, she tried to touch him, and he took a step back.

"It's okay if you've found love." She hesitated. "Have you met a girl?"

"Not a girl."

My mother, panicked, said, "Have you met a boy? A man?" She imagined that he'd suddenly discovered his homosexuality and, not knowing how to reveal it, had stayed out all night.

"No, Mamma, no. I've found God's love."

She stared at him, and her clear, small eyes quivered in the faint dawn light. She extended her hand and seemed to be about to say something. Ibro turned and ran off. Mamma climbed back up the stairs, flung the bedroom door open, and stopped at the foot of the bed. My father looked at her, his head askance. Her body and voice were shaking.

"What's the matter? Tell me."

"He's gone crazy," she managed to say in a low voice.

"What are you saying?"

"He's gone crazy," she repeated until the truth of her words sunk in. My father pulled on his pants, went down the stairs, and found him sitting on the ground outside the front door, talking to himself.

"Ibro," he called. "Come inside."

Ibro turned and fixed his gaze on him.

"I don't want to see you," he shouted before darting down the street. My father followed—Ibro running and Babo chasing behind. A group of guys was standing in the middle of the square. Ibro approached the biggest one, an Albanian, who smacked him around as soon as he laid eyes on him. My brother ran off again.

When my father reached the Albanian, the guy said, "Your son ruined my party last night."

"He's not well," Babo said. "He's not well. Don't take it out on him if he does something wrong," he added, as Ibro kept running and shouting to the guys at the top of his lungs, "It's all your fault!"

68

"You need to get a job."

I'd taken Ibro out to eat. I was in my first year of residency; the work was demanding, and in the last few months, I'd seen very little of him. We were having lunch in a pizzeria in Brera on a bright early-December day, the kind that makes your cheeks sting from the cold. We weren't city kids and felt uncomfortable among the luxury shops.

"You're so beautiful, Aida," he said once we were seated.

"Stop it." He was embarrassing me.

"But it's true, you're the most beautiful girl I've ever seen."

He hadn't been the same after London, as though fate were lying in wait to change his life forever. I was convinced that he needed structure, something to clearly mark the line between order and disorder. A job would fix things, help stabilize him.

"You don't want to finish school, and that's okay, but you can't sit around all day and do nothing."

He looked at me and started singing the chorus from a Lady Gaga song.

"Ibro, not so loud!"

The people sitting nearby stared at us and snickered. He winked at me and kept on singing. I wanted to laugh, even if I could tell that something wasn't right.

"Why don't you look for a job? At least that way, you and Babo would stop pulling each other's hair out."

"Why doesn't he give me a job? Did you know that he's put Samir on the books?"

I said nothing. Samir and Uncle Tarik had been working for my father for years.

"Babo helps everyone but us."

I thought so too, but it hurt me to hear it said aloud.

"It's not that he doesn't love you. He's just like that." I didn't know if I was saying this to him or myself.

My mind went back to when Ibro had come searching for me in the library a few months earlier. It was the end of summer, and I was studying for an exam. I only noticed him when he was standing right in front of me, crying.

"What's wrong?" I'd whispered as I walked him to the vending machines. He let me drag him along without making a sound, just a sniffle every now and then. "Did you argue with Babo?"

He shook his head.

"So what's the matter?"

He didn't answer, and the tears continued to flow. I gave him a handkerchief embroidered by Mimì.

"I can't stop crying."

"How long have you been like this?"

"Three days. More or less."

I tried to think of something to say, anything to reassure him. "You're just tired."

"Are you sure?" He was distraught, as if expecting me to provide the answer to whatever was deeply troubling him.

"I'm sure."

"Did you read it in a medical book?"

"You've bottled up lots of tension, and now it's coming out like this."

The tears didn't stop, but he seemed relieved. "I haven't slept for three nights."

"Come to my place later; I'll prescribe something for you."

He rolled his eyes.

"It's what a lot of people take, something strong to help you sleep and make you feel better."

I'd made a mistake, not as a sister, but as a young doctor. I gave him a box of Valium, and he took it as directed. He slept for four nights straight. I thought I'd fixed everything, but then came London, and now he was right there, opposite me, staring at the pizza he'd cut into thin slices, all alike.

"Aida, you've got to help me."

His eyes were shining; he was gripped by a strange frenzy.

"Eat or it'll get cold."

He put a slice of pizza into his mouth and swallowed it whole. "I've got an idea."

I stared at him.

"I've designed a pen."

I didn't know whether to be happy or alarmed.

"This time I'm going to get rich. But to sell it, I have to make a prototype, and I need the money. Can you ask Babo? He'd never give me a nickel." He was excited, almost shouting. "Aida, please, it's super important."

I hadn't spoken to my father for at least three years; Ibro seemed to have forgotten that. "Lower your voice," I whispered.

He looked around and only then realized he'd gotten too worked up. A couple near us couldn't take their eyes off him.

"Everyone thinks I'm crazy."

I felt an achingly fierce pain. "You're not crazy."

He was looking down.

"Ibro, look at me; you're not crazy."

A tear rolled down his cheek.

"You're just stressed out. Because of the school thing."

He wiped his eyes. "Do you really think so?"

"Of course, that's all it is."

He smiled, and in that moment, I believed it too; it was just a temporary phase that would vanish in a few months.

"You must have a drawing of this pen somewhere."

He brightened up. "I don't have the right things at home. I'd like to make a sketch first."

"There are plenty of paint shops around here. After lunch, I'll buy you what you need."

"You're the best." He was fired up.

"Let's finish eating first."

By the time we got up to leave, he'd mentioned at least three other things he wanted to do—illustrate comics, write a novel, and build houses with Babo. I suggested he write down all his ideas so he wouldn't forget them.

"You're right, but let's go to the paint shop now." He waited for me outside, while I paid the check.

Outdoors, the cold woke me up. Ibro was smoking a cigarette, with his earphones on. The music was very loud, and he was keeping time with his head. I called out to him twice, but he didn't answer, didn't even look at me. It was as if he were locked inside a soundproof room. I tapped his shoulder. He jerked around.

"Don't touch me," he shouted.

"At least turn the volume down," I shouted back.

"I don't want to hear them!"

I grabbed his arm. "What don't you want to hear?"

He gave me a rabid, desperate look. "These voices; they never leave me alone. I can't take it anymore."

I couldn't console him; paralyzed with terror, words like *depression*, *hallucination*, and *delirium* came into my head. I did all I could to push them aside and pretend that nothing had happened, shifting the conversation back to the pen and how important it was for him to draw a prototype. He looked at me as if he'd woken up from a bad dream and smiled.

At the paint shop, he chose the most expensive sketchbook and two boxes of oil paints, which he would then forget on the subway the next day.

Once we were back on the street, in the harsh still light of winter, I took him by the arm and drew him close. “Are you happy?”

“I am, I am, I am!”

He stepped back, sprang into the air like a released rubber band, and did a scissor kick of pure joy and strength. I laughed out loud.

69

During the day I was absorbed in my residency, but at night, before going to sleep, I always thought about him. Occasionally, I called my mother.

"Why don't you persuade Babo to hire him, like he did with Samir?"

"Because your cousin *goes* to work. One minute, Ibro says he wants to do this, and the next, he wants to do that, then in the morning he won't get out of bed."

"If Babo hired him, like he did with the others, I'm sure . . ."

"Aida, putting him on the books means that Babo pays his taxes, pays everything, and when Ibro doesn't show up, he loses money."

They refused to understand that simply indulging him would be enough to make him see reason. They only thought about money, and that made me furious. We could never seem to break free from concerns about it; it was the cornerstone of our lives. For my parents, to talk about understanding, love, and attention was superfluous.

I hounded her so much that my mother finally agreed to convince Babo to hire Ibro. For a month, things went smoothly, and even his mood swings eased. Then overnight, he gave up, just as he'd done with school.

"What do you mean he can't take it?"

"That's what he says."

I didn't understand, and her answers were no help. My father hadn't complained or scolded him, which worried me even more.

One evening, Ibro was sitting at the table. He'd just lit a cigarette when he stubbed it out in the ashtray, still whole.

"Why are you throwing it away?" my father asked. Ibro had the habit of smoking only half a cigarette, so the packs ran out quickly, and this made Babo fly off the handle. "Do you know how much a pack of those costs?"

"That sucks," Ibro replied, without even looking at him.

My father slapped him, a razor-sharp blow. My mother's lips were trembling. She was holding a pot of boiling soup, imploring Babo with her eyes. Ibro kept a hand on his cheek, as if it might fall to the ground.

"You'll never get another thing from me," Babo barked.

Ibro smiled. "I'll just ask Mamma."

"If I find out that you're giving him money, I'll throw you both out of this house," my father hissed. He stood up, and Ibro charged him, shoving him in the chest. Mamma clasped her hands over her mouth. The pan dropped to the floor, the boiling soup splashed on her legs, and she screamed. Babo fell and hit the back of his head on the door jamb. Ibro was immediately on top of him, straddling his body, a hand pressed against his throat. Babo was gasping for air.

Time stood still.

Ibro looked at my father, as if he only then recognized him, and released his hands. Then he dropped to his knees beside my mother, sobbing and hiding his face in her apron. She was sobbing too. Babo left the house without making a sound.

70

We'd arranged to meet outside. The sky was overcast and milky. Even though I was wearing a heavy coat, the cold was biting my legs, creeping up to my bum.

"Do you want me to come with you?"

I looked at Mimì, and for the first time, her face seemed unfamiliar.

"It's better if I go on my own."

I'd told her and Franco about the incident. They'd been wise and measured, as usual, but their presence would have complicated an already delicate situation. Missing a morning in the ward troubled me, but Ibro deserved the focus and emotional stability that I believed only I could provide. After the attack, I'd realized that I had to take matters into my own hands, even if it meant making peace with my father. I'd contacted the CPS, the local center for mental health, to set up a consultation, and the psychiatrist wanted to meet with us.

I looked up, and tiny shards of ice landed on my face. It was a dry, dusty sleet, almost invisible. I took a deep breath and let the frosty air drift to the bottom of my lungs. The light was dazzling. I closed my eyes to let go of the tension.

When I opened them, Mamma and Babo were there, walking side by side, Ibro following behind, his earphones plugged in. He came running over, gave me a hug, and brought my hands to his cheeks. Then he lifted me into the air.

"Let go of me; you'll hurt yourself!"

I laughed; he was always doing wacky things. When my parents reached us, I was overwhelmed with anxiety and didn't know what to say or how to behave. Should I pretend that we'd never gone through the hostilities of the past few years?

My father looked at me and held out his hand. "Hi, Aida."

He was lost. I choked up.

"Hi, Babo. Hi, Mamma." I wanted to erase everything that had kept us apart all in one go but instead headed toward the entrance.

From the outside, the building that housed the Mental Health Center resembled a nursery school, with floor-to-ceiling windows that overlooked a small garden. Once we were inside, someone led us to a large room on the ground floor, with a desk under the window and six or seven chairs scattered around, and asked us to wait there. My brother arranged four of them in a semicircle in front of the desk and sat in the middle. He smiled at us; he seemed happy. I'd told him twice where we were going, but I wasn't sure he'd understood. I sat next to him, our parents on his other side.

The snow was falling more heavily, settling softly on the bare branches. There was a moment of quiet, the first in a long time; it felt as though we could all be together peacefully. I looked at Ibro; with his eyes glued to his phone, he searched for music, still smiling. Mamma put a hand on Babo's arm. All of a sudden, I found myself missing them. My old life was reemerging through my senses—the smell of my bed, my father's smiling eyes, his tough skin, the taste of Mamma's food. All that I'd run away from was coming back, chasing after me.

The psychiatrist entered the room, introduced herself, and shook hands with each of us. She had a file with her. Over the phone, I'd explained the reason for the consultation; maybe she'd kept a record. As soon as she sat down behind the desk, I wondered what I was wearing. In the morning, I'd chosen what to put on, thinking it was important, but in that moment, I couldn't remember.

She made sure we were okay, then she asked Ibro some general questions about how he spent his days. He answered without looking at her.

"Let's talk about school. Why did you drop out?"

"I didn't like it."

"So what do you like?"

"I don't know."

"Then what don't you like?"

"Babo sent me to a technical school to become a surveyor, but I didn't want to do that."

She looked at my father, then at my mother. "And what would you like to do?"

"To write."

As she took notes, she whispered, "So he has interests, but the family doesn't support them."

In my parents' simple language, that sentence meant they had done something wrong. She was encouraging Ibro to stand up to them and them to think they were responsible for his problems. I should have spoken up, but I felt I was being watched, as if I had a hidden flaw and she was trying to find it.

"Listen," Ibro said. She put down her pen. "Something happened the other night."

He didn't know how to go on, so she smiled encouragingly. "You can speak freely here."

"I had a go at him." My father kept looking down. "But he hit me first."

The psychiatrist looked at my father's large, strong hands; they could lift and break and hammer. Then she observed my brother, as if searching for signs of violence on his body. I wanted to grab all three of them and take them out of there. My mother was crying. "He didn't mean to hurt him. It's just that, you know, he doesn't work and spends all day at home."

"It takes two to fight." The psychiatrist's remark cast a chill over the room. That woman showed no empathy for my parents. She turned to Ibro again, cutting us off. "So we'll meet here once a week. Is that okay with you?"

"Okay."

"And we'll get started with the medication too. Agreed?"

"Okay."

She dismissed us. In the next session, she'd only be seeing him.

I let them go out. "Can I ask you a question?"

She looked up from the papers she was putting in order.

"Who's going to check that he takes the medication?"

"Your brother is an adult; no one can force him to do what he doesn't want."

I didn't understand. "What's wrong with my brother?"

She smiled, a bit condescendingly I thought. "It's what all relatives ask, but as things stand, I'm not ready to make a diagnosis. And it would give your brother a label, which would be very difficult to get rid of."

So she didn't want to share her diagnosis with me because it would label Ibro forever? But that was already the case. Ibro dwelled in a state that could hardly be called normal. Her reticence was only a way to stall for time, to avoid taking any responsibility. I wondered if she was the right person, if therapy with her would be a support for Ibro; doling out the blame wasn't as clear-cut as she'd made it seem.

I went outside. The temperature had risen, and the snow had turned to muddy water that clung to my shoes, soaking them through. Ibro was listening to his music at full blast, dancing in place. My parents were standing, waiting.

"So what do you think?" Babo asked. They wanted a word that could help them understand and see the way forward, but at that moment my mind was blank.

"I need to think it over. I'll call you soon."

I waved goodbye and left.

71

My brother's body was sound, vital, ready for the world, and yet something hidden beneath the surface was holding him hostage. No one would ever say he was ill, and our eyes refused to see him as a person in need of help. So we dragged on, day after day, fending off the blows with no plan, no strategy. People can live with certain disorders, take medications, fine-tune the doses according to age, changes in weight, shifts that occur over time. Ibro, though, failed to follow through with the prescribed antipsychotics. When he took them, they put a stop to his hallucinations and aggressiveness but constantly left him in a sedated state.

"That stuff is destroying me. It's got thousands of side effects," he shouted at my parents if they tried to force him. He had realized that the medication affected him sexually, and he was still a virgin. His life was slipping away, and he didn't know how to hold on to it, so he wept, consumed with rage. Once a month he received a mandatory injection; he knew that if he refused it, they would compel him to go into a hospital. But he wouldn't take the pills. Every morning, he put one in his mouth, held it under his tongue, and then stuck it inside the bathroom cabinets or in tissues or the trash. Smoking joints gave him some peace for a few hours, except he didn't always have the money for that.

At night, he paced back and forth in the house, stamping his feet and raising his voice, getting my mother out of bed. "Ibro, please, there are people below us."

"You're right," he said, and sat on the sofa. She went back to her room and, five minutes later, heard his heavy steps again, like a jammed grandfather clock.

Sometimes, at three in the morning, he'd start singing at the top of his lungs. Once, he didn't sleep for a whole week.

My mother was at the neighbors' doors every other day. "I know he's noisy; I'm sorry."

"You don't have to apologize. It breaks my heart to hear that he's not well," the lady downstairs replied.

We plodded on, as we tried to contain the situation and understand him at the same time, unable to do either.

At some point, he started to drink; my mother found bottles hidden in shoeboxes. At night, he'd come home in a frenzy, wander the house, finishing a pack of cigarettes in a couple of hours, then go to my parents' room.

"Do you have a cigarette?" he asked my mother.

She said no, but he badgered her. "It's not true; you keep them hidden and won't give them to me."

He sat on the bed. "If I can't sleep, then you won't either." And he talked and talked about anything. My mother listened, observed, tried to be patient. My father pulled her aside. "You can't always give in to him; he'll drive us nuts."

"Damir, we have no choice."

"I won't live like this," he replied. "Don't you see that if we let him do whatever he wants, it'll become a habit and he'll always wake us up at three in the morning?"

Babo treated the issue as if it didn't concern him, until Ibro started picking on Mamma. Then he'd come to her defense, and the two of them would end up fighting.

"I'm going to throw him out of the house," my mother said whenever we spoke on the phone, and I didn't know if she meant Ibro or Babo.

I should be more of a support, I thought, but I had my own life, and my residency was demanding. I brooded over how to help him, an obsession that drained me, to the point that when he appeared unexpectedly, I didn't know what to say or how to handle him. I looked at him and no longer saw my beloved brother, only the dangerous mess I'd patiently built a wall to shut out.

72

In the spring, he started with books. Detective novels, parapsychology, then Dante, the Bible, the Koran.

"Ibro, forget it. You're too confused; you're trying to read things that require a clear mind," Babo said. Ibro would lock himself in his room and learn entire sections by heart. They were difficult texts, written in an elevated, symbolic language. I wondered what they would become inside his head. He always carried the books with him in his new backpack, a gift from Aunt Mejra. He liked staying at her place; it was his "yard time" away from our parents.

Every now and then, he came to see me at Franco and Emilia's. He spread out all his books, creased and filled with erasures and rewritings, and tore out the pages and mixed them up.

"What do you do with them?" I asked one day while I watched him cut and paste the pieces.

"I take the Koran and the Bible, erase what I don't like, and write something that weaves them together—a new book."

He wanted to rework what we were now and what we'd once been. His illness was the fault line of our lives, split between a here and a there.

My mother feared he'd become a fundamentalist. I tried to reassure her, saying that at least he'd stopped drinking. He didn't touch alcohol and obsessively checked that everything he ate—cookies, sweets, chocolates—was free of it. Believing in something and respecting its teachings gave order to his foggy, extreme states.

"I don't know, Aida," she said on the phone. "It's good to know the prayers and some verses of the Koran, but nothing more than that. The Koran is like a supermarket; you take what you need and leave the rest. There's plenty of room for interpretation."

I'd never have thought that she might take a step back from religion—she, the one who'd ruined my adolescence with her prohibitions and castigations. And while Ibro climbed trees and babbled on about being God, I watched him and laughed, and at the same time I felt guilty, because I saw in him the beauty of being alive, but a beauty intertwined with illness.

What I remember of those months is an all-consuming fear—that my parents wouldn't be able to cope, that he might harm them or someone else or himself. I agonized over how to behave but never came to a resolution. By then, my work as a doctor had taken a back seat; I was struggling with my residency, and everything was falling apart. At night, I closed my eyes and thought that his life was ruined, and the sense of injustice was so strong that it kept me awake.

73

Until we managed to get him to take the drugs, we would cycle in and out of hell. For a few weeks he'd be delirious, then he'd fall into a state of depression that could last up to a month. I buried myself in my books, trying to find a way to help him, anything to make the phases less acute. He needed to establish consistent routines, but first I had to raise my parents' awareness, since the families of patients also need to be educated. And things with the psychiatrist weren't going well.

Babo had asked her to meet with them; he wanted to find Ibro a place in supportive housing. That day, I had a midterm exam and hadn't gone along. I stopped by their apartment in the late afternoon and found them sitting on the sofa, one next to the other, my mother with her bag still around her shoulder.

"Where is he?"

"At Aunt Mejra's."

They were despondent.

"How did it go?"

Babo looked at me. "When you get there, they line you up and treat you as if you were the patient. They call you a 'case.'"

"What do you mean?"

"She said, 'You're quite a case yourself.'"

I said nothing.

"She always stares at my hands and face and never once looks at your mother's tears." He felt that she was judging him.

"Did you ask if she could find supportive housing for him?"

I didn't want Ibro to stay with them; they were constantly at loggerheads, and I feared he wouldn't make any progress.

"She said they tend to keep the patient at home, in their own environment. Then she blamed me and said I have to improve my behavior. She thinks we want to get rid of him."

The psychiatrist was passing the ball back to my parents, because she had no idea how to handle the situation either.

My mother burst into tears. "I pray every night that they take him away. Because he's aggressive, and I'm scared. They don't know anything. You can take care of a son who's sick in bed till the very end. But I can't help my son when he's like this; I don't know what to do. They're waiting for him to hurt himself or someone else. And I know it's going to happen."

Babo hugged her, and she buried her face in his shoulder. I looked at my parents. My love for them was again within reach. It was in the houses where we'd lived, in our dark, violent blood. I wanted to cry, so I ran into the kitchen to make some tea. I took it to the living room with some cookies, and we drank it in silence, as if words could pierce the thin veil of intimacy that had settled over us.

"Sometimes I think your brother is doing this out of spite, to get revenge for something. Then I come to my senses and realize it's the disease. But I'm always lagging behind. I figure out today what I should have done yesterday."

It was the first time I'd heard my father speak like that. My mother took my hand. "What upsets me most is that he suffers, because he knows what's happening. He has his moments, but then his head clears. And it's torture to see."

That evening, I felt they'd reached the limit of what a parent's heart can bear.

74

I'd only been driving for twenty minutes, and Ibro was already hounding me. "We went the wrong way."

"I'm telling you, this is the right way."

"It can't be in the middle of nowhere. It's got to be near a supermarket, a shopping mall, something."

I was smoking, my left hand out the window. The sunlight beat down on the windshield; in an hour the air would be warm. My father sat next to me without speaking, every so often glancing back to check on him.

Eventually, we'd decided to try supportive housing, although the psychiatrist had advised against it. She used his aggressive behavior as an excuse to avoid finding him a place, so I'd done it myself. The people I'd contacted told me that we needed to find the right time for him to move in, when there was no one he could come into conflict with. They also had to consider the established dynamics of the group.

In the end, I found a housing facility a few miles from Crema willing to let him stay for a trial period. They assured me that he would work and take part in a variety of activities. The monthly fee was considerable, but my father agreed to it without batting an eye.

Ibro was enthusiastic, and I felt an instinctive tenderness for him. Who knows if my father felt the same way; perhaps I could have seen the answer in his eyes, but I preferred not to look.

On the highway, I took the exit they had suggested, and we arrived without a problem. I had a look at the building, four attached colorfully painted units. My brother jumped out of the car.

"Watch out; don't get run over!" I shouted. He stopped and began hopping up and down.

"I've got to get my body moving." He did five or six push-ups, and Babo and I laughed.

The entryway was covered in yellowing tiles. An old fat woman in a faded nightgown was sitting in a wheelchair, smoking. We waited about ten minutes before someone came to get us, and during that time, she did nothing but repeat the same things and light cigarettes. Many of the patients were old, some in a semivegetative state, others with obvious signs of dementia. It was more crowded than I expected.

Ibro introduced himself to everyone. I felt a knot in my stomach. Maybe if he'd been sick for decades it would have been easier, but it had all happened so quickly. For me, he was still the lively, eccentric boy from a few months ago. My father looked terrified; I squeezed his arm.

A woman in her forties emerged from the end of the corridor, introduced herself as the manager of the center, and showed us to her office. She explained to my brother how the community worked, how many people it hosted, what he would do. "Once a week, we go to a nearby farm to help the farmers. You'll see; you'll like it."

I pictured him in a stable amid a pile of cow dung, my brother, the one who obsessed over cleanliness and ironed shirts.

"Then there are the daily activities, the swimming pool, the football field, and a running track." She was making a list of what was on offer, and I thought of all the days when he woke up and didn't want to do a thing. Then I reassured myself; they would know how to deal with him.

"Ibro, what's upsetting you?"

The question came out of the blue.

"My mother and father; they're on my back all the time," he didn't hesitate to reply. A grimace of pain appeared on Babo's face.

"My room is too small. I need a table to draw. Am I going to have a room all to myself?"

"The rooms here are pretty big."

"Great!"

"But you won't be alone; there will be four of you."

He looked at her without saying anything.

"Maybe down the road, we'll see about moving you into a double."

He sprang to his feet. "Let's go see it."

The manager led the way down the bright, bare corridor. The room was large, with a single bed in each corner, two closets, and two desks along the walls. Nothing was out of place, yet it gave off an air of neglect.

Ibro liked it. "Which one is my closet?"

She opened two doors for him, and he put his things away at once.

"Where does my computer go? I don't want anyone to steal it."

She pointed to a desk.

"And the washing machines? Where are they?"

"I'll take you to look at them later."

My brother grinned. That place would be better than staying at home with my parents.

We left him there. In the car, looking out on the dull, still horizon, Babo and I cried the whole journey home.

After a week, Ibro called. "Come get me."

They'd left him hanging around with nothing to do for days. The activities the manager had described were often suspended because of a lack of personnel, so instead of happening weekly, they took place monthly. If he hadn't been crazy already, he would have soon become so. My father left work and drove there immediately. We asked ourselves a thousand times if bringing him home had been the right thing to do.

75

"Aida, I'm going to throw my computer out the window."

He called me at the end of my pharmacology class. I went out while the professor was wrapping up his lecture on the adverse reactions of certain compounds.

"What do you mean?" I whispered, still in the room, getting nasty looks from my colleagues in the back row.

"They're not listening to me." He was agitated and slurring his words.

"Where are you?"

"On the balcony."

I looked at the soft light cast by the sunset. The day had been crystal clear, and I imagined the view from the eighth floor of my parents' apartment.

"Where are Mamma and Babo?"

"In there."

"Get inside right now. It's still cold, and you'll catch something." That year we were having a warm spring, but I didn't want him to be alone on the balcony in that state.

"Ibro, are you there?"

"Yeah."

I could hear him breathing heavily. "Go back in the house."

"I'm not going back in there."

It would take me at least an hour to reach them, maybe more; it was rush hour, and the roads were already clogged. “Do you want Babo to take you for a walk so you can blow off some steam?”

“If Babo comes with me, yeah.”

I asked him to put my father on the phone.

“Can you see what your brother’s like?”

I couldn’t tell if he was frightened or resentful. “He said that if you take him for a walk, he’ll calm down.”

No reaction from his end of the phone.

“Are you going to take him out?” I heard him sigh, hold his breath, then nothing.

“You can bring him to the square and the two of you can walk somewhere.”

“I can’t take it anymore.”

Don’t give up now, I thought.

“I can’t take it,” he repeated, as if he could sense the anger compressed into my silence.

I closed my eyes and saw Ibro walking on the balcony in a feverish state, behind him the sunset igniting the endless landscape.

“Keep him calm. I’m coming over.”

I hung up the phone before my father could reply.

76

Stuck in traffic, I watched the snake of cars spilling out from the city's outermost ring road. Beyond that, a flat expanse of fields, rows of high-rises, swarms of mosquitoes in summer, and mist three hundred days a year.

I was still trying to believe there was a reason, a real cause that would justify Ibro's altered states. My mother had gone to Bosnia for a few days, so it was the first time he'd been alone with my father.

The body of her brother Hajro had been found in the mass graves near her village. Not whole, but in fragments, one bone at a time. Before the war ended, the graves had been uncovered, the bodies dismembered by bulldozers and transported fifteen or twenty miles away. Then, these second graves were also uncovered and emptied, to fill others even farther away. The secondary and tertiary graves were used to intermingle the corpses and prevent an accurate count of the dead.

In Mamma's village, they had been separated and moved three times, so my uncle's body was in pieces. After they discovered the first bone, they waited until they'd found enough others to make an inventory of the skeleton and try to reassemble it, at least partially. Each one had been recovered, washed, dried, photographed, and cataloged. It had taken five years from the initial discovery. The denim jacket was still intact.

None of us was prepared for the terribly painful search for the missing people or the exhumation of their bodies. It was as though we couldn't come to terms with the past and had to live with the hope and fear that the ghosts of those we believed dead might suddenly reappear.

Mamma had left immediately for Bosnia, to sign the identification papers and bury her brother, at last. She'd reopened Grandma Anja's grave and placed what was left of Hajro on top of the coffin, all but a silver chain that she wanted Ibro to have. She returned to Italy directly after. A few days were all it took to put an end to a twenty-one-year wait.

Her brief absence, or maybe the discovery of Hajro's body, had unsettled my brother. Or perhaps he'd simply gone off the rails again and we had to find a way to bring him back to his senses.

In the elevator, watching the floor numbers light up, I heard the screams getting louder and louder. When the doors opened, he was standing in front of me, blue in the face, breathing heavily.

"What are you doing out here?"

He stared at me without responding; he hadn't even heard me. I approached him cautiously, as you would an animal you don't know. He bellowed, a kind of desperate growl. I was shaking. I'd never seen him so out of control before and was afraid he might hit me.

"Babo," I called softly.

My father appeared at the door, my mother behind him, like a shadow. He was ashen, but firm. There was no urgency in his movements; the situation was part of a routine. I wondered how they had managed to cope for so long. Ibro turned to my father.

"You!" he shouted, pointing at Babo. "Tell her what you do after work!" He looked at our mother. "He and all his colleagues go out whoring! Men are exploiters! Women are saints, children are saints, we must revere them! Protect them!"

Babo was speechless.

"And you are not a good mother; you never have been."

Mamma's eyes grew watery, then the light in them faded.

"Aida."

Now it was my turn.

"You left me here, by myself. I hated you, but then I understood."

He was hurling back at us all that had gone unsaid, the hidden, secret things that frightened us and grew insurmountable in our persistent silence.

"They took their money, their help, whatever served their purposes, and gave you away, and now it can't be fixed."

He took a deep breath, exhaled, releasing all his tension, and leaned against the wall. Ibro was spewing out raw chunks of undigested experience, and we took in the weight of every word, as if we were using his illness to settle the score and move on.

I stepped toward him. My cousin and uncle emerged from the stairwell. When he saw them, he ran into the apartment, screaming. Samir and I looked at each other and jumped to go after him.

77

"I'll ride with him; you follow us in the car."

I got into the ambulance. He was strapped to the stretcher; they'd just sedated him.

"I'm a doctor," I said when I sat down. "What did you give him?"

"An intramuscular injection of haloperidol, enough to calm him down on the way."

That evening, in my parents' apartment, he'd been running wildly from one room to another. He wouldn't listen to anyone except my cousin. To help overcome our shock, Samir began to tease him, "What are you doing standing on the sofa?"

"I want your pants!" Ibro shouted.

Samir replied with a playful look. "And why's that?"

"They have lots of pockets to stash the scraps of paper with my ideas. My poems and drawings."

My cousin took off his pants and slowly walked over to Ibro, then Ibro copied him. In the end, they exchanged pants, and we couldn't contain our laughter. That calmed him down.

I quickly said to my father, "Call the ambulance."

The paramedics arrived in no time. Speaking to him in our apartment, they were direct and firm.

"Take me away." Ibro's eyes were vacant as he surrendered himself.

When we left, everyone in the building was out on their balconies. I looked up and saw Aunt Mejra waving at me.

"Are you okay? Is everything all right?"

Strapped to the stretcher, he smiled and gave a thumbs-up. "Just great."

With my eyes fixed on the tinted windows, I wondered where we were, how much farther we had to go. To see him restrained felt stifling. He started singing Guccini's song "L'Avvelenata." Ashamed, I squeezed his hand, wanting him to stop. Then I saw one of the paramedics smiling and humming and decided I no longer gave a damn what anyone thought. Strapped down and sedated, Ibro was belting out the lyrics to this song of frustration and anger. My eyes welled with tears; I realized there was nothing I could do, nothing depended on me. I could only stay with him and caress his hand, just as I was doing.

78

The waiting room was large and windowless, with plastic chairs against the walls, some people standing around. I don't know if it was the exhaustion or the alienating glow from the neon lights, but my brother's behavior no longer seemed so odd or excessive, and I started to doubt my own clarity. Maybe it had all been a huge misunderstanding, an enormous mistake. As time went by, the line between balance and chaos grew increasingly blurred.

The low hum of the room was interrupted when Ibro leaped onto a chair and started preaching against slot machines, drug dealers, the exploitation of workers, and the Western world's consumption of all the food and resources, leaving nothing for poor countries. The room was transfixed, listening to his speech. I tried to make him get down, exchanging glances with Samir and my parents. We didn't know whether to laugh or to cry. There was an outburst of applause. Ibro bowed in thanks and sat back down. Overexcited, he slapped his thighs loudly.

"All good," Samir reassured him.

"Really?"

"Yeah, forget about it." And he handed him his iPod.

My brother brightened and put on his earphones, walling himself off from the world.

Samir pulled me aside. "Aida, cut him some slack. If he feels he's not being judged, he'll relax and everything will be easier."

"I just can't."

He looked me straight in the eyes. "You can't solve the Big Problem. Don't you get it?"

I was a doctor, and he was a bricklayer, and yet he'd figured it out before me.

"Try to sit with him and listen, understand what he's feeling." He took my hand. "We need to find a different way to help, a way that's good for him too, because what we've tried so far hasn't worked."

That much was clear, even if my mind was still foggy.

Before they called us, Ibro asked me to take him to the hospital chapel. As soon as we entered, he took off his T-shirt, washed his chest and armpits with holy water, then lay down on a wooden bench to rest. I let him do it without interfering.

"It's quieter here; it's nice."

I smiled. He was right. Samir was right too; this way was easier.

When our turn came, they led us to an examining room and immediately called the consulting psychiatrist.

"This one's high as a kite," the doctor said when he saw him. "How many joints have you smoked?"

My brother laughed. "Just enough."

"Enough for what?"

"To chase them away."

Then he jumped off the bed and headed for the bathroom. We heard him muttering, talking to the mirror. There, in the presence of strangers, we could no longer minimize, pretend, or deny. The doctor suggested that he be involuntarily committed. I'd been thinking about it for weeks. I had wanted to prepare my parents, talk to Ibro. And now we were in the thick of it. Mamma and Babo were paralyzed. Samir was holding my hand.

"It will be complicated to keep him in the ward with the other patients because he's aggressive, but it's the best thing to do at the moment." The doctor sounded worried.

When my parents realized what was going on, they almost felt relieved. At least in the hospital he would be treated.

79

He was happy in the psychiatric ward. My clinical shifts were in the same hospital, and I gave him the password for the staff's Wi-Fi. He downloaded movies and TV series and watched them in bed with his earphones. I asked him not to tell anyone, yet every time a new patient came to the room he whispered, "I've got the hospital password." Then he wouldn't share it because it was a secret, and he knew how to keep secrets.

When I was on my rounds, he'd call me.

"Aida, could you maybe bring me a cream-filled croissant from the café?"

Sometimes they'd run out and I'd phone him back. "There aren't any."

"But can't you find some?"

"I looked, but there really aren't any more. So what do you want? A cappuccino or a coffee?"

"A coffee. But make sure it's nice and hot because it's always lukewarm when it gets here."

I got it from the vending machine outside his ward so it wouldn't get cold on the way. It was a strange life, our life in the hospital. We established a new intimacy among people who were strangers. In psychiatric wards, all kinds of patients are housed together: anorexics, psychotics, schizophrenics, people with bipolar disorder, catatonics.

Looking around at them, Ibro would say things like "Everyone here is losing it," or "This one doesn't speak," or "The guy in the bed at the end doesn't understand a fucking thing."

He wanted to differentiate himself from the others; there was something touching about his determination.

His admission to the hospital had been difficult; they'd had to restrain him.

"If you were in my place, I'd do anything to get you out of here. I'd free you," he'd shouted angrily before the sedatives took effect. In that moment I thought of giving up, because I couldn't help but take his side, whatever that might mean. Then he calmed down, and so did I.

In the mornings, he slept, groggy from the drugs. My parents visited in the evenings, and I tried to stay with him in the afternoons. Sometimes we went to the courtyard on the ground floor to smoke.

"Can you leave me the whole pack?" I gave him a sideways glance.

"You're beautiful, Aida. You're stunning. One day you'll be in charge of all the hospitals."

I burst out laughing and handed him the cigarettes. "Hide them well, because they just might search you."

He winked at me, and we smoked without talking for a while.

"You know I can run away from here?"

I froze. I was the one who'd taken him out of the ward; I'd vouched for him.

"Don't look at me with that face. I don't want to run away. Here, I have nothing to worry about; nobody breaks my balls. Mamma and Babo are always on my case, and this is my vacation away from them." He tossed the lit butt away. "I want peace and quiet. I want to be on my own and read. Forever."

Living with my parents, moving in and out of the house, the expectations, being with other people—it was all too much for him.

"Do you know what I really need? A guide, someone to tell me what to do. Then I'd be calm, without having to think."

He looked at me. "Do you want to be my guide?"

I must have blushed. He tugged at my sleeve. "Let's go up; I'm tired." His mind was already someplace else.

He crawled into bed and dozed off. I looked at him; despite the fatigue and the agony of being sick, he was glowing, more handsome than ever. I opened the notebook he kept on the tray table beside his bed, pages crammed full of small drawings and symbols, here and there a legible sentence: "We have eternity to be together," "Were they aliens, the lights that came to you that day? But you thought, if they're coming, let them come. And unafraid, you turned your head."

"What are you reading?"

I showed him the sheet of paper.

"You don't believe in them, do you?"

"In what?"

"In aliens."

I didn't know what to say. Every time he had these delirious outbursts, I froze.

"You don't believe I'm God."

I looked at him, hoping that at any moment he'd laugh and say, "It was a joke; I just wanted to get your reaction." Instead, he pressed on. "You disgust me; you don't believe I'm God."

I didn't want to upset him; I knew he'd fly into a rage. "Listen, Ibro, I'm not good with these god things. If we draw or write or invent new words, then I'm all in, but I really don't know what to say about God."

He stared at me with wide, animated eyes, then smiled. "I want to draw a portrait of you."

"Of me?"

He nodded. I sat for him.

"No need. I know what you look like."

Without glancing my way, in less than a minute he drew a face: a child in profile, her hair lifted by the wind. Me at six years old, fleeing the war. He handed it over and clicked his tongue.

"Now I want to go to sleep. I'm tired."

He closed his eyes, and I stood there watching him in a moment that was mine alone, while the low sun shed its light over the city and softened all the edges.

80

The next day, I finished work at noon and went straight to see him. I wanted it to be a surprise; if he'd been sedated, I'd have waited for him to wake up. I peeked into the room. The bed had been made, and his things were gone. A crushing weight pressed on my stomach.

"They discharged him."

A woman in her seventies was sitting on a chair next to a man who was asleep. "They moved us to this room after they discharged your brother. The nurse told me. She said, 'We can't have two aggressive patients in the same room.'"

My brother is not aggressive, I automatically thought, but I didn't say anything, and she continued.

"This time he checked himself into the hospital voluntarily." She pointed to the man. "We didn't bring him the groceries at the usual time, and he went berserk. He has his habits, you know, and heaven forbid you should change them one iota."

I leaned against Ibro's newly made bed.

"The neighbors called us. When we got there, he'd already packed his bag. 'Take me to the hospital,' he said." Then she sighed, as if letting go of her exhaustion. "He's been like this since he was twenty. He's forty-three now."

The man was resting peacefully.

"I'll tell you something that will sound cruel. It'd be better if he was dead. This is not a life; it's just slow, continuous suffering. For him and for us."

I answered her without thinking, "Ibro isn't always like this; he just has his moments."

She stood up and took a piece of paper from the drawer of the tray table. "Here, it's your brother's discharge letter. He left it on the tray. I thought someone would come. I put it in here so it wouldn't get lost."

I opened the letter, read it, folded it up, and put it in my bag. "Thank you."

I was standing in the doorway, livid, my head throbbing wildly. She delivered that speech because she'd most certainly seen what was written on the paper. That old woman had instantly known what we'd been skirting around for months. My brother was an adult, and none of the doctors or psychiatrists who had treated him were required to inform us. I know their conversations were confidential, yet someone should have taken us aside and told us that he'd never get better, that our life would never go back to how it was.

With all these things in my head, I flew down the stairs at the risk of breaking my neck, sobbing uncontrollably, while the discharge letter burned a hole in my bag.

~

I found Ibro at my parents', in his room, busy drawing and listening to Eminem at a low volume.

"Hi, sis."

I handed him the paper. "Do you know what this says?"

He didn't take his eyes off the drawing. He'd filled the whole page with lots of colors. "Paranoid schizophrenia."

His words broke through the floor, and my heart plummeted into that deep black hole.

"I'll take the medications. Now sit down. Let's draw."

I took off my jacket, shoes, and bag and picked up a marker. Tears rolled down my cheeks, blotting the shaky lines I made on the paper. At times, he passed me a handkerchief. In the end, I said to myself, *There's nothing we can do,* and I calmed down. Until that moment, schizophrenia had only been a possibility to consider. Now suddenly, this was the reality, and we were not ready for it. We'd spent months blindly thinking that sooner or later we'd get the old Ibro back, while everyone around us knew that the old Ibro no longer existed.

81

I took a week off from my residency and asked him to come stay with me; Emilia and Franco were going to the beach. I wanted to spend time with him, see if there was another way to deal with what was happening, and give my parents a bit of a break.

My father brought him over. They showed up with two huge bags full of books. When he emptied them on the table, I saw that there were several from the library, stained with food and some pages torn out.

"And the missing pages?"

"I needed them; they were important."

He was busy arranging his things, not paying any attention to me.

"So I'll leave him here with you," my father said at the door.

"Okay, Babo. I've got this."

He smiled, relieved.

Once we were alone, I momentarily felt lost. I'd made so many plans, but now that he was with me, I didn't know how we'd fill the hours. I thought it best to leave him be. He shut himself in his room and spent the whole day reading. I avoided knocking on his door, even when he didn't show up for dinner. I ate alone and left a plate for him in the microwave.

The next morning he said he wanted to go out.

"Where do you want to go?"

"For a walk."

The sun was shining. He was walking beside me and, despite the heat, jumping on and off the low walls.

"See, I'm doing parkour," he said, excited, as I looked at his grazed knees.

When we stayed home, we drew or chatted; he liked to play with words, inventing new ones, creating rhymes. By the middle of the week I was worn out, and yet I was starting to enter a world of thoughts and sensations I'd never ventured into.

The day before he went back to my parents', while I was washing the dishes, he said, "I'm in love."

I wiped my hands on my apron and looked at him, standing in the doorway.

"Her name is Riri."

"And where did you meet her?"

"In the supportive housing."

I was surprised. "Have you seen each other since then?"

"We never saw or heard from each other again."

I thought there must not have been anything between them; maybe this woman didn't even know how he felt about her.

"I don't know what to do."

"Do you have her number?"

"I've got her email."

"So write to her."

"But she won't even remember me."

"It doesn't matter. Let her know that you're thinking of her. She'll be pleased."

"Really?"

"Hold on to this love; just the fact that you feel it is great."

He hugged me so tight it took my breath away.

That evening I looked for Riri online; it wasn't a common name, and maybe something would come up. As soon as I hit return, the screen filled with images of Rihanna. Riri was Rihanna. I closed my eyes and cried. I had believed that he'd fallen in love, that he would at least be granted that sliver of life where your heart races when you hold someone's hand. But no, that brutal disease cut him off from everything. Or perhaps I was crying for myself, because despite the reality, I still wasn't ready to give up.

The following morning at breakfast, he said, "I have to do something, Aida. Can you help me?"

"It depends."

"Can you lend me some money?"

"What for?"

"I have to go to Los Angeles."

I put my cup down. He had a sly glint in his eyes.

"I have to go see my girlfriend."

"Who?"

"Rihanna."

I couldn't tell if he was joking or just had a few screws loose. He laughed, and I thought he realized he'd said something absurd.

"She has stunning legs."

"Who?"

"Rihanna."

"Well, they're a bit big."

"You don't get it; those are real legs. You think only thin women have beautiful legs. You're wrong."

"You're definitely in love." I gave him a pinch and he laughed again. "Anyway, it's going to be tough to find the money to send you to Los Angeles."

"But you'll take me to her concert in Italy?"

"Sure."

He stroked my hand with a soft, almost impalpable touch. The light streaming through the window lit up his face, and his eyes sparkled with flecks of gold.

The intercom rang. I thought he'd get anxious at the idea of going home, but instead he ran to his room to stuff his pile of books into the bags. He came back with shorts on, barefoot.

"Do you have any socks I can wear?"

I could only find long ones in Franco's drawers. He pulled them up over his knees.

"You look like a German tourist."

He looked so ridiculous that we laughed until we cried.

When Babo walked in, he found us in stitches on the floor, holding our bellies.

82

My parents had planned to take him to Bosnia in August. I would stay in Milan and use the summer to get back on track with my residency. I'd missed a lot of classes and clinical hours but still hoped to catch up.

"Aida, we're thinking of going to South America. What do you say?" Franco threw this out over dinner one evening, taking for granted that we'd go together. "Peru and Bolivia. I've seen some incredible photos."

I struggled to find the words to tell him I wouldn't go. In the past few months, it was as though a transparent curtain had fallen between us; we managed to see but not reach one another, not anymore. I couldn't get Ibro's words about the adoption and everything else out of my head. I knew the issue didn't boil down to mere opportunism, and yet the trust between us had frayed.

"I'm staying home this summer."

Emilia seemed about to speak. Franco got up and flung open the French doors that led to the balcony. "Aren't you hot too?"

No one said another word. It pained me to hurt them, and yet there was a sense of inevitability in what was happening. For the first time in more than ten years, I felt close to my parents and didn't want to do anything to undermine our fragile connection. But this wasn't the only truth. I was also tired of always having to feel ever more grateful. That account could never be settled, so I drew on the slight resentment I felt, a remnant of all the chaos that had come before. I didn't know if they understood, but at any rate, they left without me.

As I wandered around the empty, stifling house in my underwear, attempting to study, I got regular news from abroad. Photos of skies and high-altitude deserts from one place, descriptions of mishaps that made me smile but also worry from the other.

My parents had taken Ibro to an exorcist, against my advice. Samir drove them. It was evening, and they ran out of gas. Ibro got furious and, according to Mamma, shouted so loud that even Allah could hear him. He railed against Samir and my father, "You idiots! I told you to check the gas!"

They arrived at the witch doctor's late at night. He made my brother lie down on a table underneath three suspended light bulbs. At some point, Ibro said he'd seen a cloud rise up and shatter the bulbs. And actually, they had blown out.

As a doctor, I refused to believe a word of this. As a sister, I listened to my parents tell me that on the very next day, he was a changed person.

"He's calmed down and doesn't even smoke cigarettes anymore," my mother said on the phone. "He stays home with us and wants to be cuddled like a child. He's gone back to being reasonable. This morning he woke up early and made breakfast for everyone."

I listened without speaking, knowing this was just one of the many faces of the disease. And perhaps my mother sensed this, because she added with resignation in her voice, "But even like this, it's not normal. He's not himself."

I lay on the bed in the suffocating heat, my thoughts whirling. Maybe in the absurd situation where we found ourselves, that nonsense had led to a bit of peace, like two negative numbers that when multiplied together make a positive one. The cloud before his eyes was his illness, and seeing it materialize had helped him.

83

A week after their return to Italy, Ibro was still calm. I didn't want to believe it, yet there he was, in front of me, not jumping on tables, not screaming, not singing at the top of his lungs in the middle of the street. He was stroking Uncle Hajro's silver chain, which he hadn't taken off since Mamma had given it to him.

"I've started having nice dreams again. Before, I only had horrible nightmares," he told me over a coffee, in a café behind my parents' building.

"I'm so pleased." I touched his hand. "Do you know that Samir is leaving? He's going to work in Germany."

I wanted to see his reaction, afraid that my cousin's departure might upset him.

"I know."

"Are you sorry?"

"Yes, I really am. Aren't you?"

I was sorry too, but in a different way. Samir was an anchor for Ibro. He never told me, but I think Samir had agreed to leave after his wife pressured him. She'd been driven to exhaustion and could no longer tolerate Samir going out at night to search for my brother; she wanted to put distance between them for the sake of her marriage. I wasn't resentful; I'd seen my brother at his worst and knew the havoc he could cause.

"Listen," I said, and he looked at me. "Do you want to come stay with me for a while?"

"At Emilia and Franco's house?"

"No, in a place all our own."

He smiled in a way that even now moves me. "I do, I do, I do." He lifted me off the ground. "I love you, Aida; everyone should have a sister like you."

During those months, I'd felt guilty, as if I could have done something, but had always shied away. In Emilia and Franco's empty house, I realized that, for the time being, he was my life. I would put my residency on hold for however long it took and search for a more suitable way to live with his illness. I wanted to make him take the medications, to stabilize and cure him.

84

"Aida."

My mother's voice came from far off, or maybe I was dreaming. I moved the phone away from my ear to check the time. 4:38.

"He's not well; you've got to come over."

In a matter of seconds, a rush of adrenaline coursed through my body, and my heart started pounding.

"What's wrong?" I asked, already on my feet and preparing my medical bag.

"He'd disappeared—your father went out to look for him but couldn't find him anywhere. He's just come home, covered in bruises with words scrawled all over his back."

The image of his battered body flashed before my eyes. I thought, *Srce moje*—"oh, sweetie"—*he must have picked a fight with someone.*

"Try to keep him calm. Talk to him, let him smoke."

"I don't know how. He's pacing back and forth, and his eyes are frantic."

"Keep him indoors until I get there."

In the night's stillness, Emilia had heard me talking and rushed to my room. "Darling, is everything okay?"

"It's Ibro. I'm going to my parents'."

She put a hand to her cheek. "Poor thing." She watched me while I got dressed. "What's he done now?"

"I don't know."

When I was at the door, she pleaded, "Don't drive too fast."

And she waved goodbye. She didn't want me to leave. She'd never admit it, but she was upset that I would rush off at four in the morning to drive to their home. She felt the exclusive bond between us was loosening and knew there was nothing she could do.

The road was speeding past—all around, a calmness and silence that made me shiver. I reached the front door and flew up the stairs. The lights were on, the door to the balcony wide open, and he was compulsively walking in and out. My parents were standing there, staring at him.

"I asked you to keep him calm." They looked at me; they had surrendered. Maybe I should have given them something too. "You could have talked to him, tried to . . ."

I wasn't able to finish the sentence because Ibro had seen my medical bag and immediately understood. He hugged me, then burst into tears. I thought, *Oh, dear God, how I wish I could help you.*

He let us take him to his room, then lay down on the bed and gave me his arm. Tears were rolling down the side of his face; he smiled, and his eyes narrowed into slits of joy. Someone had scratched his cheeks, the knuckles of his right hand were scraped, and there were cigarette burns on his neck. I swabbed the grazes and burns with a cotton pad before disinfecting the crook of his arm. He let me do everything, like when he was an infant. I tried to be as gentle as possible when inserting the needle. He closed his eyes.

"Babo, I'm sorry. I behaved like an animal. I don't want to behave like that with Mamma anymore; I want to use my head. From now on, things will be okay."

My father didn't respond.

"Babo, do you believe me?"

He ran his hand over his face. "Yes, I believe you. Now get some rest."

In less than two minutes, Ibro drifted into a blissful sleep.

"The drip is set at the right speed. You don't need to do anything; just let it finish. He'll be out for quite a while, maybe till midday. Don't wake him up, and try not to make too much noise. The longer he sleeps, the better."

I realized that I'd spoken with the detachment of a doctor. I watched them; it was as if they didn't see me. Things had exploded, and on the field, the three of us were left exhausted and bewildered at the end of the battle.

We sat on the sofa; out of sheer habit, my mother went to the kitchen to make coffee. I was alone with my father.

"What happened?"

"I'm ashamed."

I wasn't sure I wanted to know.

"I'm not a good father."

I didn't feel sorry for him; we each had our own personal hell.

"I can't treat him like he's sick. My head won't let me."

"What happened?" I softly asked a second time. My mother set the tray of steaming cups on the coffee table.

"He was beating up your mother, and I couldn't control myself; I went berserk."

"Did you leave those marks on his face?"

My father raised his head. "No, that wasn't me."

"So what did you do?"

"I smacked him around, lifted him by the collar. I told him to get out, that I no longer wanted him in this house."

My mother was holding the cup in her hand; the coffee had begun to tremble in the dim light of dawn. She put it down.

"Listen," she said, looking at my father. "If there's anyone here who has to go, it's you, because I will always stay with my son, even if I have to do so on my own. If you can't take it, because of your work, because it's too much for you, you can leave. I'll stay here and put up with everything, even if I've got to listen to foul language and get beaten up."

She had been straightforward and firm and had spoken with a clarity of mind that I'd rarely heard from her.

My father was looking at her, his eyes wide. Ibro's illness was changing all of us. Or allowing us to become what we always could have been. He got up, walked to the bathroom, and locked the door. We could hear him weeping.

I took my mother's hand. Her eyes were dry; she forced a smile.

85

Peace returned to the house. Babo seemed more understanding, and Ibro was calm and affectionate again. He waited for our mother to sit with him on the sofa so he could wrap his arms around her and smother her in kisses. He no longer wanted to go out; everything exhausted him. I kept watch from a distance, hoping that phase would last as long as possible. For the first time, my parents were fully aware of his condition, and I thought this might change things.

One Monday morning, the psychiatrist phoned.

"Ibro must come here to the CPS."

"When?" Babo asked.

"This afternoon."

He gave the message to my brother, who didn't go that afternoon or the next day or the day after that.

On Thursday morning, the psychiatrist phoned again.

"Ibro's done something very serious. He's got to come see me here at the center."

"Why can't you tell me over the phone?"

"Because I have to talk to him."

"How can someone who's not in his right mind do something serious?"

She insisted that they bring him to the center. Babo had to struggle to convince my brother, but the three of them went to the meeting.

The psychiatrist was agitated and stern. "Ibro, what did you do the other night?"

My brother looked at her but didn't answer.

She turned to my parents. "The carabinieri called me."

My mother blanched.

"Why?" my father asked.

The psychiatrist shot back, "The other night your son smashed up a car window."

My father pressed him, "Is that true? Did you really do that?"

Ibro was looking outside, as if the whole thing didn't concern him. "I only wanted to sleep in the car; it was cold." Then he pulled a tissue and pen out of his pocket and started to scribble.

The psychiatrist put her hand on her brow. "Someone recognized him and filed a complaint."

"And what happens now?" my father asked. My mother was unable to speak.

"There will be a trial. Ibro must appear before a judge."

"Because of some broken glass?"

"It's a minor offense, but this is the legal process." She paused. "After a few months, the judge will issue a ruling. Your son could end up in the OPG."

My father didn't understand and neither did my mother.

"The OPG is a hospital for mentally disturbed offenders. Ibro could be involuntarily committed."

She hadn't wanted to tell my parents what it really was, but Babo guessed. "An asylum?"

My mother spun around to look at Ibro, who kept on scribbling.

"No, it's not an asylum. Anyway, Ibro, you shouldn't worry; it's the first time this has happened, and you don't have a criminal record. But if it happens again, if you aren't able to control yourself . . . In any case, as a preventive measure, we could look at putting him in supportive housing." She looked at my parents. "You could choose one you think he might like, go and see it together, then we can try to move him up on the waiting list. Or we could find a hospital, temporarily, while we wait for a spot to free up." She was speaking as though my brother wasn't in the room. "If he's already in supportive housing, the judge might be more lenient."

Now that things had gotten out of hand, she'd changed her mind about supportive housing. But after his experience in Crema, my brother no longer wanted to live in a community.

"Is there any other option?" Babo asked.

"No, nothing."

The psychiatrist wanted to be clear because her conduct would be reviewed. They sat in silence for a few minutes. The leaves on the branches shimmered in the soft autumn light; they had yellowed, their sap had drained away, and soon they would fall.

She stood up to dismiss them. "If you have any questions, call me." She turned to my brother. "This doesn't mean that our sessions or your medication will stop. I'll see you next week, as usual."

Without saying a word, Ibro smiled and put the tissue in her hand. Then he left, followed by my mother.

My father stopped in the doorway and, lowering his voice, said, "I'm worried my son might harm himself."

"He's an adult."

Babo's eyes were on fire. "Look, I live on the eighth floor."

"If you're worried, then rent a place on the ground floor."

Babo stormed off, furious and humiliated. She shut the door and turned the paper over in her hands. When she opened it she saw, written in capital letters, AFTER CPS, ASYLUM. And underneath, a drawing of a coffin.

86

The days rolled past, one after another, while we waited. Like astronauts on a mission, we were floating in space, and Earth appeared tiny and distant.

Ibro too had retreated into his own world. He'd gone back to listening to music on his earphones, cutting himself off from us. Nothing interested him anymore. He'd randomly open a book, pick out a few sentences, underline them, and then close it. He didn't want to do anything, not even eat.

On his birthday, I went to visit him. As soon as he saw me, he gave me a note. It said 20+1.

"What does that mean?"

"I've lived twenty years. This past year has not been a life."

"What's it been?"

"I don't know," he said without even looking at me. He was drifting away, and none of us knew how to handle it. We were so worn out by his extreme behavior that apathy gave us some respite. I continued to look for a house for the two of us, thinking that if I could take him somewhere else, things would change. That was the only prospect that kept me afloat.

Then, a registered letter arrived from the court. On the morning of November 13, a Friday, he had to appear before a judge. We had a real deadline to deal with; the world was once again concrete, definite.

~

I went to my parents' place with a shirt and dark sweater in his size. I'd bought them for the hearing. He wasn't there.

"Where is he?"

"At Tarik's."

My father was sitting on the sofa, my mother cleaning the kitchen. "I'll make some coffee."

It was almost seven in the evening.

"I went to Bosnia for two days."

"Mamma told me."

He was silent, chewing something. "I tried to find supportive housing for him there." I looked at him, not understanding.

"If the judge rules against him, we'll run away." I was shocked. He hadn't given up. "It's still our country, isn't it?" I couldn't help but smile. "It's a pleasant building, among the trees, a former barracks. If you want to work, you work; otherwise, you can have time to yourself. There were people collecting fruit to sell. I saw it with my own eyes."

I would have loved to hug him but didn't. It was he who, with a clumsy movement, unexpectedly embraced me. The warmth and strength of his body melted something hard inside me and transformed it into tenderness for our embarrassment, for his efforts to go beyond the limits imposed on us, for the surprise my body felt sensing his so close, for how our bodies recognized one another in spite of everything.

"We must regularly tell our children that we love them and not just caress them when they sleep," he said, holding me tight, while I tried to rein in my runaway heart.

When the door opened and Ibro entered, we quickly drew apart, as if to hide that sudden intimacy. Without even saying hi, he went straight to the kitchen to talk to Mamma. "I smoked a cigarette with Uncle Tarik."

"Okay."

"And I drank a glass of wine too."

"That's okay."

"I won't do it again."

"What harm could it do, Ibro?"

"I just wanted to break up with God."

"Why do you want to break up with God?"

He didn't respond and went to his room.

I followed him. "Look what I've brought you." I showed him the shirt and the sweater. "They're for the hearing. What do you think?"

Any other time, he would have tried them on immediately; instead, he carelessly tossed them aside and stretched out on the bed.

"Aida, do you know that I can fly?" I looked at him, terrified. "I'm like a hawk."

"Ibro, get these thoughts out of your head. Birds fly, not people. And you are a person."

He must have sensed my fear because he winked at me and smiled. "Sometimes I just say things."

There was a stillness to his calm, as though even his blood had stopped flowing.

"Are you afraid?" I asked.

"Of what?"

"Of the hearing."

He stared at the ceiling for a long time before responding. "If I make a mistake or overreact, they'll lock me up."

I sat next to him and put a hand on his arm. His eyes were clear, honest.

"Don't worry; I'll take you. We'll have breakfast, go over what to say, and then head to the courthouse."

"What if it goes badly?"

"Just be careful how you behave over the next few days, and be smart. Try not to take on the psychiatrist because she can put in a good word with the judge."

"But what if it goes badly?"

I hesitated before saying, "If it goes badly, Babo thinks we can run away to Bosnia."

He opened his eyes wide. "Really?"

And when I said yes, he burst out laughing.

Escape would be our salvation a second time, but in the opposite direction.

"I've brought you back together at last."

My heart raced. I felt the immense suffering my absence must have caused him, growing up alone, the responsibility of the male child destined to redeem a whole family, a destroyed country.

"Don't cry, Aida. It's not your fault."

I couldn't hold back my tears as he kept a hand on my back to comfort me. It was vivid, resplendent, and painful all at the same time. Like walking through fire, the beauty and light of the flames, the torture of burning alive.

~

The day before the hearing, I called him.

"I'll come pick you up early tomorrow morning."

He only managed to tell me that he was confused.

87

I was having dinner with Emilia and Franco.

A ring. I answered.

She saw that I was trembling, that my body was shaking so violently I could barely hold the phone. She drew closer, I told her, and her mouth fell open. Franco got up from the table and came to embrace me.

They took off my sweatpants, got me into a pair of jeans and a jacket. Once I was in the car, my reflexes took over. On the road lit by the streetlamps, time expanded and contracted, preventing me from counting the passing minutes.

The ambulance had come from my hospital, all people I knew. My father was there, standing, his face ashen. Doctors and paramedics were bent over the body. The one in charge of CPR didn't want us to get near; a postmortem would be necessary, and the carabinieri were checking that all the operations were scrupulously carried out.

I noticed a colleague from my specialty and yanked the sleeve of his uniform. "You can't keep me away. What the fuck? He's my brother."

He went to speak with the person in charge of CPR, then nodded in my direction.

I remember first seeing his trousers. They were ripped; the air pressure had torn the fabric in several places. Then I saw him. He was lying on his back, arms outstretched and palms facing upward, eyes half open. Smiling. The body completely intact, not a drop of blood, not even a broken tooth, only the right leg slightly twisted. It looked as though someone had lifted him up and set him down on the grass. For a second, I thought he hadn't fallen from the eighth floor. On the phone, Babo had told me he jumped, and all the time I was in the car I'd thought he was on the ground, smashed to pieces, but alive.

I knelt down and touched his head to understand how he had died. The back of it was round, smooth, undamaged. Upon impact, the cervical vertebrae had crushed but hadn't fractured. A fracture causes instant death. He hadn't died instantly. He had landed on his legs and fallen backward; it looked as though only the tibia and femur were broken. In all likelihood, the pelvis had broken too, and the internal organs had ruptured. And yet, his body still retained a perfection that I would never see again in all my years on the ward. Those who jump fall head-first, and their skulls shatter. He was beautiful. When the paramedics were about to remove his body, I took off his silver chain and put it in my pocket before they could see me. Shrouded in the cold light of the streetlamps, everything was indistinct, suspended.

I walked over to join Mamma and Babo. They were leaning against a wall. A doctor was taking Babo's blood pressure and vital signs. We looked at each other, none of us able to speak. I sat down.

"We were at home, watching TV, *Sconosciuti*, on Rai 3. You know, that program where people tell the stories of their lives." My mother was staring straight ahead as she spoke.

"He was on the balcony, smoking and listening to music on his computer. I went out to tell him to turn it down, then came back inside. At some point, I noticed the volume was still high and went out again, but he wasn't there. I thought he was sitting downstairs, like he often did. I called out to him; I knew he wasn't in the house, if he'd come in, I'd have noticed. That was when I leaned over and saw him on the ground, with his hands facing up. Then your father went down."

He continued. "I must have been screaming as I ran down the stairs because the neighbor heard me and immediately came over. When I got there, I hardly needed to touch him to realize he wasn't breathing. I didn't even try to revive him."

They spoke one after the other, their voices muffled.

"We were inside and didn't hear a thing, only the loud music coming from the balcony. Perhaps the pain was so great he didn't cry out. I think he was still alive after he hit the ground."

"Who knows how long he'd been there like that. Maybe fifteen minutes."

"He was alone; even then he was alone."

They were trembling like leaves of paper, and I feared the wind would carry them away.

Everyone from the building had come down to the street. Surrounded by the neighbors' affection, Babo and Mamma even managed to smile.

Around two in the morning, we went back inside. We all slept together in their bed, me between the two of them. I could hear them breathing. I found myself wanting to be cuddled like when I was a child, reached out and found my mother's motionless hand. It was wrinkled and weightless, like the bark of a cork tree, the fluids having run dry. All at once, I could see the lost years, the struggle to build a life, and a destiny that had turned against us, upsetting everything. I wondered how anyone could survive their own life.

I felt a great warmth in my chest; my love for the two beings breathing alongside me was as immense as the stars.

Old Ibro was right; he had brought us back together.

His death was a supernova.

88

The next day, Babo and I went to identify him in the morgue. From behind a glass partition, we looked at his body lying on a metal tray, his head poking out of the bag, in profile. I don't know if it was because I couldn't touch him, or because he was frozen in an unnatural stillness, emptied of everything, but in an instant I realized it was no longer him.

I saw the pain coming, like a wave rising and drawing near, and stayed there, letting it crash over me. I let myself fall to the ground until I felt the hard, cold floor pressing against my cheek. I sensed my father reaching to catch me, and I screamed with a voice that I didn't know I had.

89

When Ibro was born, everyone in the neighborhood came to hold him in their arms. He died as a son, as a brother to them, not just to us. We decided to bury him in Bosnia, and once the neighbors learned, they asked if we could have a funeral in Italy too, to say their goodbyes. I was astonished by how many people knew him and how many he knew. The continuous flow of visitors didn't stop until late into the night. His schoolmates showed up, as did the first volunteers who'd welcomed us, the families from the old house with the courtyard, everyone I studied and worked with in the hospital. It was as though all the things in the world opened up to reveal every last bit of the love they contained.

Emilia and Franco never left our side. My parents hugged them in the most natural way, as if there had been no years of silent hostility, of unspoken demands. Mimì frequently took my mother away from the crowd, held her hand, talked to her, caressed her cheeks. They had secrets, and that filled me with joy.

90

It took me five days to pull together the documents to get the authorization to take the body out of Italy. My brother was a non-EU citizen living in Italy; we needed birth and death certificates, a request for transportation outside the municipality of residence, clearance from the Bosnian Consulate authorizing the passage of the body and its arrival in the village, clearance from the Public Prosecutor's Office declaring his death a suicide, the mortuary passport issued by the prefecture, a certificate from the ASL, the local health authority, certifying the hygienic conditions of the body and the coffin in which it would be transported.

During the long hours spent in those offices, sitting and waiting, I thought about Ibro. I tried to imagine his face as he hurled himself forward and took flight, his nimble body, first tense, then light in the air. Perhaps he wasn't thinking clearly and had leaned too far over, or maybe he wanted to challenge fate, like when you drive flat-out on the highway and don't stop, even though you know it's dangerous and you could crash. I was trying to find an explanation, instead of accepting that I could not alter even a moment of what had happened.

I felt like I was facing war again. Nothing was within my control. The feeling of impotence made me furious, reduced me to despair. The burden was mine to bear; the reality of the situation would not change.

91

After twenty-one years, we were traveling on the same road, this time in the opposite direction, and like then, Ibro filled the space.

Babo and I took turns driving. Mamma dozed off; she'd taken something to help her sleep.

As dawn was breaking, we rounded the last bend. A powdery, icy snow had started to fall. We noticed it too late, when the wheels lost traction and the car skidded. My father jolted to attention, as if waking from a dream, and gripped the steering wheel tighter, then looked in the rearview mirror to see if I was frightened. I wasn't frightened; I wasn't thinking; I didn't feel anything.

By now we could see the first houses and the white tombstones stuck into the earth everywhere. The woods stood guard over the village, its dry fingers stretching beyond the road to embrace it. My father had wanted a *groblje*, a cemetery. *Groblji* are quite different from Christian cemeteries. They are not separate from the villages; they are gardens open to all where you can walk, so that the living and the dead can sleep close together. After the war, he'd bought a tract of land on a hill opposite our village. At first he wanted to build a school on the site, but there were no children left. The hill is a tranquil, quiet place, visible from every house. Women look out their windows and gaze upon a son, a husband, a father.

At the entrance to the village we saw a crowd of people. They were standing, in silence, under the falling snow. In the center, Ibro's coffin.

"They're all here." My mother pointed to the black spot in the distance. We knew we would find them there, the survivors. My father searched for her hand and grasped it. Without taking her eyes off the road she said, "No pain turns your heart to stone like the loss of a child. You feel frozen inside, dead."

My father let go of her hand and placed it on the steering wheel.

In no time, we were outside, and the icy air whipped our faces. Granddad came toward us, brought my father's fingers to his lips. *"Sine, sine, sine."*

Then he looked at me and my mother. He had endured many things in his life. He'd been an orphan in his early twenties, a carpenter in Milošević's Serbia, a partisan. And yet, faced with my mother's pain, Granddad could only walk past her, toward the coffin. I don't know if his knees gave way or he wanted to bow to Allah's will, but he dropped to the ground, without a sound, like one of the snowflakes falling in the valley.

I drew closer and called to him softly, "*Djedo.*" "Granddad."

I tried to lift him, but he resisted, so I crouched down next to him on the frozen ground. He took my hand and placed it on the coffin. He cried and repeated, "*Oči moji mili.*" "My dear, little eyes."

We were his beloved grandchildren, who had survived war and poverty, the little treasures he had longingly imagined from afar. It was the last time he could keep us close.

The men carried the coffin into the mosque; the *hodza*, the Bosnian imam, would then take the body, remove the clothing, wash it, and sprinkle it with perfumed oil for burial.

We arrived at our house and had to prepare small packages with fruit juice and cookies to give to whoever came to the service, a symbolic pledge that reminded people to pray for Ibro.

I closed my eyes to try to visualize Ibro and felt a blow to my chest—I couldn't remember his hands. I had touched them a thousand times, and yet I didn't remember them.

"Babo."

My father was in the bedroom, putting on a suit that I'd never seen before. He had bought it especially. "I'll wear it today, then I'll throw it away."

He was tired. The new suit was too big, making him look small, isolated from everything. I adjusted the shoulders of the jacket and smoothed out some imaginary creases, just to ensure he was really there, in front of me, and wouldn't fade away with the first gust of air. I held my breath. "I have to see him."

Ibro's body had been purified, and none of us could touch him again.

"In all the confusion of my life and the loss of . . ."

My brother's name died in his throat and came out like a gasp. He raised a hand to his face and covered his mouth, then sat on the bed; his breathing returned to normal.

"One thing I understood: my children come first."

He had used the plural, even though I was the only one left. No late awareness, no regret could bring my brother back. He pulled a pair of undershorts from his pocket. "I found them in the closet. They still smell like him."

He held out an arm for me to take them. I shook my head. "You loved him."

"Desperately," he said. I knew that Babo loved me too, but not with that same tenderness. "Aida, you've never needed me."

I had worked my whole life to be independent, because I believed this would make him love me more. Instead, it was just the opposite; it is easier to love fragility. I looked out the window in search of my brother; the curtains in my parents' bedroom swayed slightly. The muezzin had started to sing.

"*Oči moji mili*," I whispered. And I went out.

92

In the mosque, the *hodza* watched me from a distance as he prepared the mixture of perfumed oil. Ibro's body was covered with a white sheet.

"Babo said I could come."

He stared at me for a few more seconds, then motioned for me to come closer. When I was next to the body, he grabbed a corner of the sheet and lifted it. His hand was there, manicured, waxy. We hadn't been this close since the night he'd thrown himself from the balcony. I tried to touch him, but the *hodza* stopped me.

"One last goodbye," I said.

He couldn't object; it was inevitable, and human. I sat down and caressed his head, his neck, his arms, his chest. The anguish of the past few days, the swirl of questions, the pressing thoughts, the waves of resentment melted, passing from my hands to his body. Having him in front of me and being able to touch him for the last time put me at peace.

93

After the service, people came to our house. I wanted to sit in a corner and let the pain overwhelm me, but as soon as someone saw my eyes grasping at the void, they tugged me, spoke loudly, or embraced me. Ibro would have been at ease among that swarm of Bosnians.

Little time was left until the burial. Only men were allowed to attend. Without saying anything, I went to join the funeral cortege. My mother refused to come. There were fifty men, dressed in black. The ones in the middle carried the coffin on their shoulders—over it, a green sheet.

Many thought my presence was inappropriate, but Babo kept me with him, at the head of the procession led by the *hodza*, a dense line walking toward the hill. There had been a small landslide, and the snow was mixed with mud. Our feet sank into the ground. The air stung our faces and kept us alert, on the brink of despair. All around was white, silent, still.

A hole had been dug under the branches of a large chestnut tree. The displaced soil stained the snow dark. I looked away; that earth would weigh on my brother's body.

The *hodza* stopped, and the men holding the coffin lowered it into the ground. It fell to Babo, Samir, and Uncle Tarik to cover it with shovelfuls of dirt until it disappeared from sight. Then we all turned to stand with our backs to the grave. The men started to chant a low, slow note, arising from the depths of the earth, shaking the roots of the trees and the foundations of all the dwellings.

We buried Ibro, and with him the hatred, the shame, the sin of the war and our fractured lives.

V.

THE HOUSE

94

I'd just left the conference room when Paolo called.

In New York, the December wind claws at your face, so when I heard the phone I was tempted not to answer, to avoid pulling down my scarf.

"How did it go?" he asked.

"We made a couple important contacts."

I regularly attended conferences with the head physician, trying to obtain funding for a study our department was working on.

Paolo was silent.

"Are you still there? Better if we talk when I'm back at the hotel. I'm freezing."

He waited a moment before saying something like, "As soon as you get home, we have to go to your mother's." I don't remember his exact words; the din of Fifth Avenue filled my ears.

I slowed down. The other pedestrians dodged me, and I could only see the treetops whipped by the wind. I decided to walk across Central Park, even if I risked getting to the airport late. I needed time to work off the anxiety that had gripped my nerves.

95

My mother wasn't well. I was a doctor, and my husband was a doctor, and I quickly grasped that he was worried.

Babo had rebuilt the whole house back in Bosnia, three floors plus a basement. In the end, he'd only given up on the swimming pool. He'd gotten to spend a couple of summers there, before he died of a heart attack while laying a mosaic floor in an apartment in central Milan. After that, my mother left Italy for good and returned to the village, alone.

A neighbor was keeping an eye on her, and that day, she had called to say she thought something was wrong.

"What does that mean? Couldn't she have been more specific?" I asked Paolo. Vagueness irritated me.

"Aida, she doesn't even know what a thermometer is. We've got to go and find out."

My mother lived an isolated life. At dawn, she fetched water from the well. She washed little, ate little, and went to bed when it got dark. She had roughened in manner and appearance. Her only activities were to work in the garden and visit my brother's grave. Twice a day she sat under the chestnut tree, gazed at the white tombstone, and closed her eyes to pray, her palms upturned, raised to her heart.

96

Paolo was waiting for me outside, at the sharp bend in the road. Whenever he came to pick me up, I insisted that he not drive all the way into the airport. "There's no need."

"You're taking away the pleasure I get when I see you appear from behind the sliding doors," he protested. But to me it seemed a waste of time.

As soon as I sat down, he came over and kissed me on the cheek.

"Did you bring a change of clothes for me?" I'd asked him to pack a small suitcase with some comfortable sweaters, a pair of jeans, and heavy boots.

"Yes, it's all in the trunk."

I still wasn't sure that we needed to do everything so quickly, but I didn't want to argue. If it was a false alarm, I'd find out soon enough. Christmas Eve was around the corner, and we'd decided to stay at his family's. It was relaxing to spend the holiday with people I wasn't close to, or in the ward. We'd be back in Milan in four, five days at most, in time for Christmas dinner.

Paolo insisted on driving. "You've got to be jet-lagged."

"Yes, but I'm six hours behind you."

He ignored me and headed toward the beltway, having already made up his mind. I answered a couple of work emails, then fell asleep.

When I opened my eyes, the sun was sinking below the horizon. "Where are we?"

"It's not long now till the border. At the first service station, we'll stop for a coffee."

I hadn't been on that road since Ibro died. Outside the window, lights from houses in the distance and then only the dark shadows of a few frozen trees. Soon, all the blades of grass would bend in the nighttime cold, as they had back then. I looked at my reflection in the glass and saw my childhood face, and along with it, all that had come to pass.

97

We arrived as night was drawing to a close, the bleakest moment before dawn.

My mother was waiting at the top of the stairs, wearing a light-colored dressing gown, her white hair covering her shoulders. She shone a flashlight in our eyes. "Oh, it's you."

"Mamma, why are you standing in the dark?"

"Because I don't want the neighbors to meddle in our business."

It was to save money. She hadn't turned on the heating yet, even though there was almost two feet of snow on the ground.

"I've made up the room on the first floor for you; I'll sleep downstairs. If you're cold, there are more blankets in the closet. See you in the morning."

Then, like a ghost, she disappeared.

"She seems to be in fine form," Paolo said with a smile. He was used to her peculiar ways. They amused him. I was too tired to get upset.

98

When we woke up, it was noon. I looked out the window; the snow-covered forest enchanted me, as it had for as long as I could remember. I screamed the minute my feet touched the ice-cold floor. Paolo burst out laughing when he saw me hopping about; I dove back under the blankets and reached for his body. We couldn't stop laughing and didn't want to. We made love. I'd never thought it would be possible in that house, and it could only have happened with him. Paolo wasn't uncomfortable with my past. He never had been. Afterward, we grabbed our heaviest clothes and dressed under the covers.

I wandered through the house to look for my mother. Only the basement was warm, with the wood stove burning. I was sure she was living there, holed up in that room with a wall equipped as a kitchen and a bench that converted to a bed.

"Why does she insist on turning the heat off? It's a miracle she hasn't caught pneumonia."

"But it's fine down here."

Paolo looked in the fridge, scrounging around for food. On the table I found a note, written in a shaky hand with large capital letters.

"She went to Zvornik to buy meat. She says she's left the sweet cake in the oven for us and some *burek*."

He loved *burek*.

"She looks like she's in perfect health," I said, already thinking I'd made a wasted trip.

"Let's wait until we've examined her."

"I just think she didn't want to be alone at Christmas so asked the neighbor to phone us."

"We can always bring her to Milan to stay with us."

I shot him a sideways glance.

We ate greedily, and while I washed the dishes, Paolo snooped around. An old calendar with pictures of Tito and a few framed photographs were hanging on the wall.

"Here's one of you and Ibro."

I craned my neck. "Where?" I didn't remember any photo of the two of us.

"Next to the Leaning Tower of Pisa."

I came closer, my hands dripping with soapsuds. When I saw it, my throat tightened; I'd done everything to try to forget that picture. It reminded me that I hadn't looked after him carefully enough, or loved him enough, that I hadn't been able to save him. Now it had suddenly resurfaced and swept me back to the past.

"You're getting water everywhere."

I looked at the floor.

"Are you okay?"

I nodded and returned to the dishes. Paolo understood my mood swings and could manage them easily. I watched as he rummaged through a cardboard box. I'd seen the same expression on his face whenever he found something unexpected on a patient's X-ray.

I walked over; the box was full of photographs and notes in different handwriting. They were folded up, repaired with tape and organized in a way I didn't understand, into small bunches held together with paper clips. We emptied the contents onto the table; I translated them out loud.

"My name is Begsada. I was captured at a checkpoint on July 7, 1992, while trying to escape from Zepa. I was studying biology at the

University of Sarajevo, in my third year. I think I'm a prisoner in the Prijedor Camp.

"My name is Fahret. They took my son Salih. He is five, with a red birthmark on his back. I don't know where he is. I have a brother who lives in Hamburg, Germany. Here they make us sing Serbian nationalist songs at the top of our lungs all day, and if we don't sing, they beat us with guns, sticks, kicks, and fists. Whoever reads this, please don't forget us.

"My name is Mirnesa. They took me along with my two daughters. And now they rape me in front of them. Help me, I beg you, help me.

"My name is Amir, I've been in the Trnopolie concentration camp for thirty-nine days. We eat twice a week, the soldiers bring pans and jugs, they relieve themselves, and we have five minutes to finish everything while they beat us. Yesterday they raped a woman in front of us. If we have an erection, they cut off our penis.

"My name is Elvisa, I've been in the camp for . . . I don't know, I lost count. The soldiers torture us with axes, electric cables, cans of petrol, chainsaws. Every day, they pile up the bodies, mutilated, decapitated, burned. Before throwing them in the pits, they cut off the ring and pinkie fingers; we Muslims are forced to be buried with the Serbian salute on our hands. I no longer know if all this is really happening, if I'm alive or dead."

In the photos, I recognized people from the village, friends, Babo's and Mamma's relatives, Uncle Hajro. There, laid out on the table, was everything they had been made to endure, the end they had encountered. Their faces, their hands, the bodies of the people we had loved had been torn away from us by indiscriminate, chaotic violence, its only purpose to dramatize the horror.

Paolo took my hand and brought it to his lips. "It's over, Aida."

That simple gesture was enough to bring me back to the present. I was alive; he was there with me.

Mamma entered without making a sound; in the doorway she took off her shoes, drenched with snow. "Here you are. Awake, finally."

She came to give me a hug and saw the papers strewn across the table.

"Who gave these to you?" I asked.

She was touching them as if she knew them by heart. She took three photos that were clipped together. "Here, this one. Ljiljana and her children. Do you remember her? They lived just beyond your grandfather's orchard."

I imagined her on long evenings, endlessly poring over the photos, alone.

"He gave them to me, a neighbor, the first time we returned after the end of the war. Your father wasn't home, and I decided not to say anything. There was no reason to torture him too."

My mother had held on to that secret for so many years.

"You can't live in this house with all this stuff," I said.

She was looking at the photos spread on the table, fingering them lovingly. "I always wanted to get rid of them, but in the end . . . it's like they became part of the family."

Quickly, I put them back in the box and threw it on the fire. She couldn't or didn't want to stop me, and as the flames swelled, she was weeping and laughing.

99

In the afternoon we examined her. I wanted Paolo to be there because I was afraid I might miss something. While she was putting her clothes back on, we went outside to talk. It had started snowing again. The mountain was shrouded in a silence that astounded me.

"I don't like what I'm seeing," Paolo said, but it was already clear to me. "Her legs are swollen, which is odd at her age; she's not that old, and everything tires her." He was thinking about her heart. "We need to take her to Milan, do all the tests, and help her get back on her feet."

He was right, but it meant convincing her to leave the village. "She'll never do it."

"Talk to her; tell her it's not forever. Once she gets better, she can come back here."

We knew it wasn't true. But she couldn't continue to live in the middle of nowhere, alone, with the burden of that house.

"There's no other option."

Paolo was resolute and calm, like any good doctor. And like a good husband. Under the big flakes of falling snow, he gave me a hug and restored my clarity.

"I'll talk to her tonight."

100

Dinner was delicious. My mother had simmered the meat over the fire for two hours, and it had absorbed the smoky aroma of the wood.

Paolo kept the conversation lively, and my mother let herself be carried away by his good spirits; she smiled, told us about the rose garden she intended to plant in the spring, how radiant the valley was in the summer. Then she said that we were lucky, because that night we would see a total eclipse, a rare event.

Paolo got up to look at the sky.

"It's too early," she said. "We have to wait a bit longer."

"Then I'll have to miss it. I'm feeling tired from the trip and would rather go to bed."

He gave her a goodnight kiss on the cheek. "Thanks for the dinner, Fatima. It was delicious."

She blushed, or maybe it was just the heat from the stove.

Once we were alone, I started clearing the table. Keeping my hands busy helped me organize what I wanted to say to her.

"Aida, come over here."

She was standing in front of the window, looking at the sky.

"There are a few clouds, but also a good wind, so if we're lucky we should be able to see it. Let's sit here and wait."

I arranged two chairs next to each other. In the stillness, I sensed her shape, the warmth of her body. We sat without saying anything, as time seemed to expand. Finally my mother spoke; it was as though she was returning from a grueling, relentless journey.

"When you were born, I couldn't wait for you to sit up. Then I couldn't wait for you to start crawling and walking."

She paused.

"And once you learned to walk, you went away."

There was no reproach in her eyes, nor in her voice.

"Because of us. We wanted our own house, we wanted to send money here, we wanted so many things, and children don't stay young forever. All of a sudden, we discovered that you'd grown up."

She was looking out the window, in search of meaning somewhere, amid the snow.

"I saw how you ran to meet her, how you waited for her when she wasn't there, how you held her hand. I was jealous."

The image of Mimì, of the moment I saw her for the first time, came to me vividly. I gave a start, like I did then. Then I looked at my mother. How I had longed for her to confide in me in that way. And now that it was happening, the words dried up in my throat like withering leaves and fell to the ground.

"I let you go because I thought that the fears, the pain I held inside would hurt you."

I searched for her hand, squeezed it lightly. She didn't take her eyes off the woods.

"I thought, 'This way she'll be safe. At least *she* will.'"

I looked outside too, at the trees, the snow, the darkness. All was quiet and delicate. She had believed that her sacrifice would save me, but no one can save anyone. I had to learn to find peace within myself. Like her—she too had to find peace. I took the silver chain from around my neck and laid it in her hand. Her eyes quivered. "I took it before they carried him away in the ambulance."

She looked at it as if it were an apparition, clenched it in her fist, then hugged me. She held me tight and rocked me.

"*Kuca moja mila*," she kept repeating as our cheeks glistened.

Wrapped in her warm body, I found the secret of my childhood.

101

That night she slept in Ibro's room. She'd left the window open, and the thin curtain swayed back and forth, swollen by the wind.

A breath—his—must have woken her. She heard it next to the bedside table. She thought it was him because when he slept, he made an almost imperceptible sigh with his lips. She turned and saw him on the balcony. She remained still, in silence, not wanting him to vanish. Then she got up and pushed the curtain aside.

The trees stood motionless, and the stars twinkled, cold and pure. He was there, at the edge of the woods, smiling at her, his left hand raised to the height of his heart, in the ancient Bosnian sign of farewell, like Babo, like Granddad.

She went outside to look for him, her bare feet sinking into the snow. When she reached the dense tangle of branches, she saw two sparkling amber eyes lighting up the emptiness, observing her. They watched each other for a long time.

Then he ran away under the starlit sky, free. She curled up and fell asleep.

The eclipse was full, the moon only apparently dying out. In the brief convergence with Earth, it acquired a new radiance, black and fiery.

At dawn, I found her lying on the edge of the woods, perfect and undisturbed, frozen in her pale dressing gown, her white hair resting on a pillow of snow.

She was smiling. Her heart contained all the rivers, the mountains, the leaves, the clouds, the silver of our land. A land so profound that not a soul could unravel its mysteries.

Publisher's Note

If you or a loved one is suffering from mental illness or emotional distress, please know that you are not alone. Help is available 24/7 at: 988lifeline.org

About the Author

Alessandra Carati is a writer living in Milan. The original Italian edition of this novel, *E poi saremo salvi*, won the Viareggio-Rèpaci Prize for debut authors in 2021 and was short-listed for the Strega, Italy's most prestigious prize for literary fiction in 2022. Carati also wrote *Bestie da vittoria* with Danilo Di Luca and *La via perfetta* with Daniele Nardi. Her latest novel, *Rosy*, was published in 2024. *Once We Are Safe* is the author's first translation into English.

About the Translators

Linda Worrell and Laura Masini met during a workshop at the British Centre for Literary Translation in 2019 and have worked together ever since. Their translations have appeared in *The Common*, *The Southern Review*, *The Georgia Review*, and *Visible: Art as Policies for Care. Socially Engaged Art (2010–Ongoing)*.

Linda lives in the UK. Her translation of a short story by Giuseppe Pontiggia was published in *The Southern Review*.

Laura splits her time between Tuscany and Cambridge. She translated Matthew Lipman's novel *Mark* for Liguori and has contributed her short stories to various Italian anthologies.